DYING ░░░

Prophet saw movement out of the corner of his left eye. Wheeling, he felt a bullet burn his temple at the same moment he heard the report and saw the smoke and fire stab from Bannon's gun. For a split second, the smoke and fire and the burning pain in his head enveloped him. It did not freeze him, however. As if of its own accord, his right hand brought the Peacemaker up level with Bannon's chest. It jumped as it fired.

Bannon flew back against the massive, cracked wall of granite behind him, face pinched with pain. He started bringing his gun up again, and Prophet's second shot took him through the soft skin beneath his chin and out the crown of his skull, painting the granite red. What remained of Bannon toppled back toward Prophet, who stepped aside as the dead man fell face first into the dust. . . .

Prophet spat and said, "There you go, you son of a bitch," and holstered his smoking gun. . . .

Praise for Peter Brandvold:

"Takes off like a shot, never giving the reader a chance to set the book down."   —Douglas Hirt

"A writer to watch."   —Jory Sherman

THE DEVIL
AND
LOU PROPHET

PETER BRANDVOLD

BERKLEY BOOKS, NEW YORK

THE DEVIL AND LOU PROPHET

A Berkley Book / published by arrangement with
the author

PRINTING HISTORY
Berkley edition / February 2002

All rights reserved.
Copyright © 2002 by Peter Brandvold.
Cover art by Bruce Emmett.

Visit our website at
www.penguinputnam.com

ISBN: 0-425-18399-8

BERKLEY®
Berkley Books are published by The Berkley Publishing Group,
a division of Penguin Putnam Inc.,
375 Hudson Street, New York, New York 10014.
BERKLEY and the "B" design
are trademarks belonging to Penguin Putnam Inc.

PRINTED IN THE UNITED STATES OF AMERICA

10 9 8 7 6 5 4 3 2 1

For my brother-in-law,
Terry "Bubba T." Cline of Dalton, GA.
The South will rise again!

I am one, my liege,
Whom the vile blows and buffets of the world
Have so incens'd that I am reckless what
I do to spite the world.

—SHAKESPEARE, *Macbeth*, ACT III, SC. I

1

THE MANHUNTER LOST the tracks of his quarry forty miles west of Three Forks. He cursed a good note, as was his way—cursed himself, his horse, the day, the approaching dusk—then got back on his ugly, hammer-headed dun and rode hard for another mile and a half. Between a low, rocky hill and a spring, he picked up the tracks again in the mud the spring made as it trickled across the trail.

"Ha-ha!" Prophet congratulated himself. "There you are, you sons o' bull-legged bitches!"

He kicked the horse into a canter, leaning out from his saddle as he followed the tracks through a valley that deepened into a gorge, then rose into mountains, firs climbing around him on rocky slopes, the clean, fresh smell of pine in his nose. Lion scat lay on a small, saucer-shaped rock sitting shoulder-high along the trail. There were deer tracks galore.

Prophet figured he was a good two miles beyond the spring when the smell of pine sap was tinged with the smell of cook smoke. He immediately halted the mountain-bred hammerhead, the meanest—and best—horse he'd ever owned, and lifted his nose.

"Yep, that's pine smoke, Mean and Ugly," he told the horse. "Where in the hell's it coming from?"

The horse was sniffing, too.

Not wanting to ride into a camp of the men he was hunting, Prophet slid out of the saddle with a catlike grace remarkable for a man his size—six-three, two hundred and ten pounds, none of it lard—and tethered the white-socked dun to a lightning-split cedar. Peering cautiously from beneath the funneled brim of his sweat-stained half-gallon Stetson, he shucked his Winchester '73 from the saddle boot and quietly followed the shod prints of the four horses, stepping lightly so as not to kick rocks and give himself away.

The game trail he and the others had been following emerged from the pines and snaked down a ledge, twisting around granite boulders tufted with moss and split occasionally by gnarled fir roots. It planed out in a grassy meadow where a sod-and-log cabin sat about fifty yards from a barn and a corral. Four horses milled in the corral. Outside the cabin, a man was splitting wood in hide britches, red flannels, and suspenders, a blue bandanna flopping around his neck in the chill spring breeze.

It looked to Prophet like a buffalo camp or a horse outfit. By the shabby state of the buildings and corral, Prophet figured it hadn't been much of anything except a hideout for roving outlaw bands for a good five, ten years. Outlaws weren't much for keeping up appearances.

Prophet went back to his horse for his field glasses. While there, he grabbed the spare six-shooter from his saddlebags, snugging it behind his cartridge belt, and returned the Winchester to its boot. He had a feeling this was going to be a job primarily for the sawed-off, double-barreled shotgun hanging from his saddle horn by a worn leather strap.

Gripping the Richards coach gun before him, he returned to the ledge overlooking the meadow. Squatting down behind a boulder, he lowered the shotgun to his side and trained the glasses on the cabin. The man chopping wood had his back to Prophet. None of the other men appeared to be out and about. They'd had a long ride from Three Forks, where they'd robbed an express office and where Prophet had picked up their trail. The other three were probably sacked out like March lambs.

Prophet lowered the glasses and stared out across the meadow, his gray-green eyes catching the light of the west-angling sun. A grin broke across his rugged, sun-seared face with the thrice-broken nose. "Perfect. You just sleep tight, pards."

Prophet returned the glasses to his saddlebags, then made his way down toward the meadow, clutching the barn blaster out before him and weaving around boulders. He stopped several times to cast a gander at the cabin and to check on the man splitting the wood. The outlaw kept his back to Prophet, until at last he disappeared inside the cabin with an armload of wood.

By that time, Prophet was halfway down the trail. He paused behind a boulder through which a fir had grown, and scanned the meadow once again. The man who'd been splitting wood had obviously stoked the cabin's stove, for the tin chimney was belching smoke like a steam locomotive on a sharp upgrade.

"Easy, hoss, easy," Prophet told himself. "What the hell you gonna do—do-si-do in the front door and ask what's cookin'?"

He crouched, turning his back to the rock, and ran a

thoughtful hand along his jaw. How in the hell was he going to take all four of the men in the cabin without getting himself killed? It didn't matter what happened to his quarry, for the wanted dodgers read "Dead or Alive," but Prophet needed to stay above ground in order to collect the two-hundred-dollar reward per head and have one hell of a good time spending it.

He slid another look around the boulder and saw the smoke puffing from the chimney, thick white pillows of it tearing on the wind. The smell of pine was sharp in the clean, chill air. Far away, a hunting hawk screeched, and for a moment Prophet envied the bird its defenseless prey—a burrowing critter or a magpie's nest rife with eggs.

"I'll get 'em, goddamnit, I'll get 'em," he whispered reassuringly, staring at the smoke-belching chimney. A soft light entered his gaze and the corners of his mouth lifted slightly. "And I know just how I'm gonna do it, too."

He grinned and looked around for a rock a little bigger than the chimney. Finding one, he picked it up, hefted it, and stole another look at the cabin. The windows were silhouetted, so he couldn't see if anyone was looking out, but the lack of activity told him that if they weren't sleeping they were no doubt seated or reclining on cots. They had no reason to think they'd been followed. Prophet had been a good half-day behind them.

He stole around the back, where stove-length logs were stacked to the low-slung roof. Pressing his ear to the log wall, he listened. The wall was so thick he could hear little but an intermittent hum of desultory conversation, as though the outlaws were playing a casual game of cards. Satisfied no one inside was savvy to his presence, he carefully climbed atop the wood pile. From there he flung himself ever-so-daintily onto the roof, which was sod framed with wood, sliding his shotgun ahead through the grass.

Hefting the rock, he sat on his butt and pushed himself along carefully, one slow movement at a time, until he reached the chimney. Squelching a snicker but allowing himself a self-congratulatory grin, he set the stone over the chimney pipe. Only a few wisps of smoke escaped around the sides of the uneven rock. He sat there for several seconds, grinning and listening, the wind kneading his hat.

Finally, an exclamation erupted through the sod beneath his ass, followed by the muffled sound of chair legs scraping the puncheon floor. Prophet turned to crawl to the front of the cabin, where he intended to order the men to surrender as they ran out the front door to escape the smoke. He hadn't moved more than a foot, however, when the sod and wood planking sank beneath him. There were two sudden, shallow drops and the dismaying sound of splintering wood.

Prophet froze, eyes widening.

"Oh, shit."

The roof sank still further. Then it opened with a terrific crack, and Prophet went through the hole like a man falling down a well.

"Sheeee-iiiiitttt!"

Losing his shotgun, he smashed through a table covered with cards, tin cups, and whiskey bottles, and hit the floor with a crash. Men were yelling and smoke was billowing. Stunned and aching and trying to regain the wind the table had knocked out of him, Prophet turned on his side, throwing off rubble. He looked around the room, but the smoke was too thick to see anything but intermittent, moving figures staggering away from the table, arms flung over their burning eyes.

"What-in-the-hell?" one man yelled.

"Law!" another bellowed.

Above the cursing, coughing, and chinging spurs, Prophet heard the unmistakable sounds of gun hammers clicking back. The sound sent adrenaline jetting through his veins. Knowing he'd be dead in seconds if he didn't react fast, he gained his feet, hunkered down on his heels, drew one of his two Colt .45s, and fanned the hammer, jerking in a complete circle as he fired. When the first gun was empty, he drew the second, pivoting this way and that and letting go a cacophany of gunfire that had his ears ringing so loudly he could barely hear the shouts and cries of the men he was ventilating.

By the time the second gun was empty, the room was so full of smoke that Prophet couldn't breath, and his nose, eyes, and lungs were on fire. The cabin was deathly silent. He searched for the door, hitting solid wall several times before he found it, and ran out choking and wheezing, clutching his throat with one hand, his empty gun with the other.

A gun barked behind him. A slug tore into the ground a foot to his left. Turning, squinting his seering, running eyes back at the smoke-filled cabin door, Prophet saw a tall man, with a savage face and a thin beard, staggering and taking awkward aim with a six-shooter. The man's shirt was covered in red, and blood dripped down his left cheek.

He fired again as Prophet dropped to a knee, thumbed back the hammer of his Colt, and squeezed the trigger, the hammer hitting the firing pin with a sickeningly benign ping.

Prophet's pulse pounded as he remembered the gun was empty. *Both* guns were empty!

The man kept coming, staggering, choking, and squinting his eyes. He thumbed back his gun hammer and fired, the slug tearing into a corral slat behind Prophet, who dropped his empty Colt and reached for the Arkansas toothpick on his belt. He flung the knife at the approaching gunman. Because of the ringing in his ears and burning eyes, his aim was off; the blade sailed over the man's left shoulder and clattered against the house.

"Hah, hah!" the man roared. "Now what are you gonna do, you son of a bitch!"

The gun came up and barked as Prophet ducked, shoulder-rolled to his right, and came up making a beeline for a water trough.

"You're a dead man . . . whoever you are!" the bandit raged, staggering after Prophet like a half-blind madman, gun raised and ready. The gun barked again, the bullet thunking into the wood in front of Prophet, who cowered behind the trough.

Prophet's heart was racing and his ears were ringing. Hands shaking, he stuck out his right leg, jerked up his faded denims to just above his boot, and pulled the double-barreled derringer he kept in a small, homemade sheath strapped to his calf.

"I'm gonna fill you so full o' lead you'll jingle when they drop ye in the hole!" the gunman raged as he approached the trough. He fired his Colt, and Prophet felt the burn of the bullet notching his ear.

Wincing against the pain, Prophet brought up the hideout gun, forcing his burning eyes open, knowing this was his last shot, and fired just as the bandit brought his own revolver up and was stretching a scraggly grin. Prophet's slug took the man through the throat, making a penny-sized hole. The man froze, his eyes widening. Automatically, he dropped his gun, bringing his hands to his throat. He was as good as dead, but to finish him, Prophet fired another round through the man's forehead.

The man staggered sideways, took one step back, and fell on his face, sighing as he expired.

Prophet stared at the man through his burning eyes, then at the cabin. Smoke billowed through the open door. Strings of it trailed out of the new hole in the roof. His shotgun was in there, but he'd wait for the smoke to clear before he retrieved it.

Prophet sighed and looked around like a full-grown man newly born, trying to gather his wits. The past few minutes had passed so quickly and intensely that now, with it all over and finding himself still alive, he wasn't quite sure what to do with himself. His ears still rang but the pain in his eyes was abating.

Never a man to go long with unloaded guns, he sat on the edge of the water trough and thumbed brass into the chambers of his two Colts. As he worked, his swirling thoughts slowed steadily into backwaters, and he became aware of a numbing pain high in his back. Flexing his shoulder daintily, he realized he must have separated the damn thing when he'd fallen through the roof.

"Goddamnit," he cursed, twirling the cylinder of his second Colt. He'd found through considerable experience that a rope and a strong horse worked rather well at popping bones back in place.

Prophet shook his head and started for the barn. The big man sighed.

"Helluva day."

2

PROPHET WOKE THE next morning, turned on his sore shoulder, and groaned with pain. He felt like someone had hammered a dull rail spike deep in the joint.

Opening his eyes, he stared around the cabin, half-hoping he'd find himself in the Waddy's Cottage in Henry's Crossing, clean sheets beneath him and the smell of breakfast emanating from the kitchen downstairs.

No such luck. He was lying on a spindly cot in the ancient cabin, the morning sun glaring through the four-by-four-foot hole in the roof, beyond which occasional birds fluttered. As his vision cleared, he saw the blood splattered on the walls and smeared on the floor, making several gruesome trails to the door and outside.

He'd dragged the bodies out last night, after he'd jerked his shoulder back into its socket and the smoke had cleared. He'd decided not to head for Henry's Crossing until morning, as his arm had been too sore to lift the cadavers onto the horses. Also, the trail was dangerous at night, haunted as it was by roving outlaw bands and renegade Indians.

He'd boiled coffee over an outdoor fire, eaten some jerky and stale biscuits he found in his saddlebags, and used a few tips of his whiskey bottle to relieve the pain in his shoulder enough to conjure sleep. He'd slept rather well, too, in spite of the shoulder, the ceaseless yammering of coyotes and wolves, and the coppery smell of blood in the cabin.

Throwing his blanket aside, he swung his legs to the floor, stomped into his boots, donned his hat, and headed outside, working the kinks out of his neck. Gazing across the shabby yard, which the morning sun had discovered and painted a soft gold, lightly brushed with a fuzzy breeze, he inspected the bodies laid out side-by-side before the corral. The outlaws' horses stared at Prophet across the prone, blanket-covered figures of their former owners, as if to say, *So what now, hotshot?*

Prophet's shoulder barked at the mere thought of wrestling those bodies onto their mounts, but that's exactly what he had to do. He couldn't wait around here another day. His grub was low, for one thing, and this was outlaw country, for another. Bounty hunters and outlaws rarely mixed without fireworks.

He approached the bodies, squatted down, and threw the blankets back from the pale faces, belligerent-looking even in death. He recognized McTeague and Clawson, having cowboyed with both down on the Staked Plain one summer. The other two—a burly, middle-aged hombre with a long gray beard, and a tall, stringbean fellow with receding blond hair and hand-tooled Texas boots— he didn't know.

Hoping he hadn't made a mistake, he reached into his shirt pocket for the descriptions, and let out a sigh of relief. Since he'd turned to bounty hunting six years ago—after having tried everything from soldiering and scouting to bartending, cowboying, riding shotgun for a stage line, and even wearing a deputy sheriff's badge for a year—he'd had nightmares of drawing down on the wrong man, one of the many hazards of the job. Witness descriptions were not always accurate, and neither were the pen sketches on wanted posters. And Prophet would have been the first one to admit, if only to himself, that he got a bit careless at times, having been raised by a Georgia cotton farmer who believed the best way to approach any obstacle was head first. You could reflect once the dust settled.

In bounty hunting, however, the slightest mistake could put you on the wrong side of the law in a heartbeat, make you a target of your own breed. Odd how that made the job both nasty and compelling, Prophet thought now, stuffing the papers in his pocket. He knew it was not to his credit that he liked doing what he did, and he could understand the revulsion of others. But there was just something dangerous enough about it to make every other job look dull.

And like his old man had said—foul-mouthed drunk that Silas Prophet was—you're dead one hell of a long time.

"Well, there's no time like the present," the bounty man said as he headed for the barn, where the outlaws had put up their tack.

He dreaded the nasty job of lifting the bodies onto the horses but was eager for its completion. When he got to Henry's Crossing, he'd stay there awhile and pay a whore to coddle him with whiskey and lovin'. Maybe he'd go down to Mexico, spend a few months by the ocean. He'd heard the señoritas were something special, cheap as snakewater but sweet as sugar. Hell, maybe he'd even find another line of work—in Texas, say, where the winters weren't so harsh. Something less revolting but equally interesting. Maybe he'd even find a woman to settle down with. Hell, stranger things had happened. . . .

Saddling the horses was a big job in itself, straining Prophet's shoulder. Several times he considered leaving the tack, but couldn't do it. He knew that if the dead men's kin didn't claim them, which they probably wouldn't, he could sell them to a livery barn, upping his take-down by as much as a hundred dollars. Prophet was many things, even a spendthrift at times, but he'd been barefoot-poor enough to never turn his back on an extra cent.

Saddling the horses was a job, but getting the dead men onto the horses, even with the help of his horse and lariat, about made him faint. That railroad nail he'd woken up with had doubled in both size and number, and they were tearing around in his bruised shoulder, probing for nerves. The morning was cool, but he sweated like a butcher, and by the time he was through, his face was as pale as the cadavers lashed to their horses.

He boiled coffee and took his time sipping it and eating the last of his jerky and biscuits, waiting for the hammer in his shoulder to ease its pounding. It did so after about twenty minutes, and Prophet kicked sand on the fire, returned his coffee pot to his saddlebags, and mounted the ugly dun, heading out, leading the four horses, tied tail-to-tail, by a rope.

The day warmed quickly, and as he headed east, the sun was warm on Prophet's stiff, aching shoulder, which he couldn't wait to soak in a hot tub and hire a pleasure girl to knead gently with her fingers, caress with her naked breasts. Mile after mile, he thought about those fingers, those breasts, a tall glass of pilsner, fresh tobacco, and a bottle of Tennessee whiskey. To pass the time, he hummed and occasionally even sang a few bars of songs from his Confederate past: "Jeff Davis built a wagon and on it put a name, and Beauregard was driver and Secession was the name . . ."

He made it to the outskirts of Henry's Crossing at midday, halting the string of horses on a chalky clay butte overlooking the town, a collection of primitive buildings scattered about the little yellow shack that did duty as the ferry office. Like many Western towns, Henry's Crossing had been spawned by river traffic and the intersection of several freight roads.

At the moment, Gil LaBlanc's ferry was leaving the town side of the Missouri with a big Murphy freight wagon and four mules, the ferry bucking the waves and taking on water like a half-submerged tree. In town, a terrier tied outside the mercantile was barking at two kids teasing it with sticks.

Prophet hiked a leg around his saddle horn and rolled a cigarette, giving the horses a breather after the long climb up the butte. He studied the big painted letters— WADDY'S COTTAGE—on the side of Henry's Crossing's only hotel—a thirty-room affair with a veranda on both the lower and second floor, and the best cook this side of the Rockies. The woman who owned the joint, Ma Thurman, was the most persnickety bitch you'd find north of the Pecos, but she ran a tight ship, nearly bedbug free.

Thinking of those beds, and the whiskey and women over at the Queen Bee, Prophet heeled the roan, jerked on the lead rope, and started down the trail into town, sucking on the quirley until it was no longer than a thimble, then tossing it in the well-churned, clay-colored dust of the trail.

". . . and Beauregard was driver and Secession was the name . . ."

He rode past the boys now sitting on the boardwalk chewing candy, past the tinware store and butcher shop and a half-dozen drays parked before the sawmill which filled the air with pine. He crossed the board bridge over Mud Creek and pulled up before the little mud-brick shack with a weather-beaten shingle announcing simply "SHERIFF." He climbed tiredly down from the roan, clamping his jaws as another lightning bolt shot through his shoulder.

"You kids stay away from those horses," a man behind him ordered.

Prophet turned to see a bandy-legged little man, with snow white mustaches and worn wool trousers held up with a pair of snakeskin galluses, crossing the street in front of the Excelsior café. Wearing a tarnished silver star above the pocket of his blue-plaid shirt, Sheriff Harlow F. Fitzsimmons frowned at the two boys who had been teasing the dog. They'd been attracted by the blanketed bundles on Prophet's horses, and were heading this way.

"Are those dead men, Sheriff?" one of the boys asked, eyeing Prophet's bundles.

The sheriff stopped in the middle of the wide, dusty street and aimed a crooked finger at the kid. "I told you to git!" His voice was as high-pitched as an old woman's.

The boys turned tail and ran back toward the mercantile.

The sheriff walked up to the last horse in Prophet's string and lifted a blanket. "Can't you come in the back?" he snapped.

"I didn't know you had a back door," Prophet said.

"I don't, but you could tie the horses back there, then come around the front and get me. You have to make such a goddamn spectacle?"

"Well, I got 'em covered this time, for chrissakes!"

"And watch your goddamn mouth! There's ladies shoppin' in town today."

Prophet mopped his forehead with a cuff of his sweat-soaked shirt. He was used to being received this way by tin stars like Fitzsimmons, or "Little Fitz," as he was known by the townsfolk. "All I want is my money, and I'll be on my way."

Fitzsimmons shoved his hands in his pockets and approached the bounty hunter suspiciously, his washed-out blue eyes going over the taller man as if sizing him up for a hanging. "These the ones held up the express office? Where'd you find 'em?"

"Down in Horsetail Valley. There's an old buffalo camp out there."

"You backshoot 'em?"

"No, I didn't backshoot 'em!" Prophet protested. He would have been the first to admit he wasn't the most scrupulous of bounty men, but he didn't go in for backshooting. He took pride in that and was thoroughly indignant that anyone would suspect otherwise—even "Little Fitz."

"Well, how'd you bring down all four of 'em, then? They musta been sleepin'."

"No, they're weren't sleepin', neither." Prophet hesitated. "They were, well . . ." He slid a glance at the wrapped bundles on the four horses, trying to come up with a reasonable explanation that wasn't too terribly far from the truth. He knew that if anyone found out he'd fallen through the roof of the outlaw shack, the story would spread faster than cheap whiskey to every saloon in the Beaverhead. He'd never live it down.

"There was a hole in the roof," he explained finally, with an air of haughty indignance. "I saw that from the hill above, and I decided to use it to my best advantage. That's how you stay alive in my line of work, Sheriff.

You use whatever they give you . . . you use it *against* 'em." That last sounded even smarter than Prophet had intended.

Fitzimmons cocked his head and squinted one eye skeptically. "The roof?"

"I jumped through the roof, landed feet-first on their poker table, and caught 'em with their pants down. I ordered them to drop their irons, but as you can see"— he turned to the bundles on the hang-headed horses, two of which were drinking from the trough along the boardwalk—"they didn't take my advice." Prophet pursed his lips, so satisfied with the story that he was eager to tell it to the girls over at the Queen Bee.

The sheriff rolled his eyes and shuffled toward the door of his shabby office. "Come on, Prophet," he grumbled. "Let's get to the paperwork. A hole in the roof, you say. Huh!"

The paperwork would have taken five minutes if the sheriff had been faster with a pencil and hadn't had to spell every word aloud before he wrote it down. When he finished, he set the pencil aside with the air of a difficult job well done, folded the reward request, and dropped it in a desk drawer.

"Well, you know the drill, Prophet. It'll take a few days for the express company to process your request. I guess you'll be waiting around for the money." Obviously, the prospect of Prophet's remaining in Henry's Crossing did not appeal to the aged lawman, who scowled and gave his head a sharp sideways jerk.

"I reckon, Sheriff," Prophet said. He enjoyed antagonizing the old coot, who wore the badge only because no one else wanted it. He was about as effective at keeping the peace in Henry's Crossing as a broken-down nag would have been, but fancied himself the next Wyatt Earp. Deep down, Prophet didn't mind. It was ineffective lawmen like Fitzsimmons who made the pickings rich for bounty hunters.

"Don't worry, I'll mind my p's and q's," Prophet said, like an unctuous schoolboy, squeezing the old man's shoulder. "Wouldn't want to cross a man with your sand."

"Well, see that you don't!" Fitzsimmons barked as Prophet headed for the door. "If I have to turn the key on you, it might be a while before I turn it back again."

"I hear ya," Prophet said, throwing up a wave as he stepped outside.

He was riding off down the street, in the direction of the undertaker's, when the sheriff called his name. Befuddled, Prophet turned around, and Fitzsimmons beckoned him back. Prophet shrugged and reined the dun back to the jail, where the sheriff stood gazing indignantly across the street.

"I forgot," he said grudgingly. "The sheriff over to Johnson City sent you a letter a few days back."

Prophet was incredulous. "A letter?" Prophet was friends with Owen McCreedy, the sheriff of Johnson City, but couldn't imagine what he'd be writing him about.

"That's what I said." Fitzsimmons turned into his office. He reappeared a moment later and offered Prophet an envelope which had already been opened. Prophet glanced at the sheepish-looking Fitzsimmons and removed the letter. It read:

Dear Proph:
Time to call a favor in. Please find a showgirl named Lola Diamond and bring her to me by the 19th. She's traveling in your area, with Big Dan Walthrop's Traveling Dolls and Roadhouse show. Should be in Henry's Crossing soon. I need her for

*questioning at a court hearing. Find enclosed $150
for your trouble and $15 for two stage tickets to
Johnson City.*

> *Hoping like hell you'll take the job,*
> *Your pal,*
> *Owen McCreedy*

Scowling, Prophet folded the letter and returned it to
the envelope. He looked at Fitzsimmons. "What's it all
about?"

The sheriff shook his head. "Don't ask me. McCreedy
didn't tell me much more than he told you. Just said he
needed her there in six days, which is gonna be a problem
since her troupe ain't due in here till the fifteenth, day
after tomorrow."

"Why don't you just tell her the law wants her, and
let her find her own way down to Johnson City?"

"My guess is she won't go unless she's got a . . . uh . . .
escort, I guess you'd call it." Fitzsimmons smoothed his
mustache with the thumb and index finger of his right
hand, wagging his head dourly. "Don't ask me what ol'
McCreedy has goin' down there, but it sounds to me like
he's got his hands full. Otherwise, he'd send his deputy
for her. Instead, he's got you . . ." He chuffed without
humor and shook his head once more.

Prophet lifted his hat and scratched his head. Mc-
Creedy's cryptic note befuddled him. Its desperate tone,
and the fact that he owed McCreedy a favor, was making
it hard for him to turn the job down—in spite of his
exhaustion and aching shoulder. He and McCreedy had
once ridden for a cow outfit in western Kansas, and the
favor Prophet owed McCreedy involved the ranch owner,
his daughter, and the lie McCreedy had told the man to
save Prophet's hide.

"She gets in day after tomorrow?" he asked Fitzsimmons thoughtfully.

The sheriff nodded. "Her troupe's due to play here again in two days. She's a redhead. Pretty. Big blue eyes and a figure that . . . well, you can't miss her."

"I'm not so sure I want to find her," Prophet groused.

"Well, that's up to you and McCreedy. I don't want no part of it. Downright unprofessional, you ask me. Sendin' a bounty hunter after a murder witness. Ain't even sure it's legal."

"Why don't you do it?"

" 'Cause I'm needed here, for godsakes!" Fitzsimmons defensively exclaimed. "The goddamn city council hasn't hired me one single deputy. Not one! If I took this little . . . this . . . *tart* . . . down to Johnson City, hell, not only would my wife prob'ly leave me, but the town would be burnt to the ground by the time I got back. What with all the rivermen and owlhoots and soldiers on the prod every day and night—"

"All right, all right, I get the drift," Prophet said, thinking it over.

Taking a showgirl down to Johnson City shouldn't be such a hard way of making a hundred and fifty dollars. Hell, he'd been planning to head that way anyway, as soon as he'd pocketed his reward money and rested his shoulder a few days. He'd heard the gambling was good down there, and the whiskey and women were even better. Why not repay an old friend a favor and get paid for it?

The decision must have been apparent on Prophet's face. When he lifted his eyes from the boardwalk, he saw that the sheriff was holding out an envelope. "You're to serve her with this here subpoena. I reckon it's legal, but I won't vouch for it. Like I said, this is between you and McCreedy."

"A showgirl, eh?" Prophet said, ignoring the paper and staring at the false front of the Queen Bee with a shit-eating grin on his face. Hell, he'd tracked renegades through deserts for little more than a hundred dollars. Even with a sore shoulder, how hard could it be to accompany some showgirl down to Johnson City? Prophet could catch up on his shut-eye between relay stations.

"A right purty one," Fitzsimmons said, slapping the subpoena against Prophet's chest. "And a right ornery one, to boot . . . or so I've heard."

"Ornery, huh?" Prophet said, taking the paper. "Will I have your help corralling this little tomcat in the stage?"

Fitzsimmons's eyebrows furrowed and his chin lowered. "Uh . . . well, I'd like to help you out there, Lou. Really would. But if the townsfolk see me helpin' a bounty man cart off a showgirl . . . well, you know . . ."

"Guess it wouldn't look too dignified, eh, Sheriff?" Prophet said sardonically.

"Well, dangit, a lawman has to look professional, you know. And I have a feelin' more than one or two people around here aren't going to want to see . . ." Fitzsimmons ended the sentence abruptly, looking off and gritting his teeth as though he wished he hadn't said as much as he had.

Prophet thought he understood. Handling the girl would no doubt require finesse. Some of the men in town would probably try to intervene, if they had the chance. Not to mention the people the girl worked for. But Prophet, unlike the hapless Fitzsimmons, knew how to work around such obstacles. He'd been doing so for a good many years, and prided himself on his cunning.

"Well, it's about a two-day stage trip," Prophet said. "I reckon we can start after I've collected my fee for these hombres—and still get to Johnson City by the nineteenth."

"The show's supposed to be through the weekend," Fitzsimmons warned tauntingly, "so you're gonna make her and her handler a might angry."

"Well, I guess I should expect to put up with a *little* hardship," Prophet said, trying to get the old man's goad as he started off again with the horses. He smiled and shook his head.

But as he stopped and waited for a passing string of freight wagons, he pondered the fact that, while he'd tracked enough thieving and murdering men to fill a good-sized prison, he'd never hunted a woman before. Especially a showgirl with a good many surly fans, not to mention a male handler or two. On the surface, such a job appeared relatively easy. But Prophet knew from experience to look beneath the surface . . . and he wasn't sure he liked what he saw.

Besides, he didn't like the desperate, cryptic tone of Owen McCreedy's letter. Prophet knew there was a lot the sheriff of Johnson City hadn't told him, and he wondered why.

As he headed down the street, he turned a look behind to see Fitzsimmons staring after him with a big coyote grin on his face.

3

TWO DAYS LATER, Lou Prophet awakened in the Queen Bee to see a lovely brunette standing naked before him. Biggest tits he'd ever seen, much less squeezed.

"How in the hell old are you, anyway, Sally?"

The girl looked at him as she bent over to step into her bloomers, the enormous breasts hanging straight down before her like oversized hot-water bottles. Her face paint was smudged, her hair was a mess, and sleep lines creased her face, but she still looked glamorous for a whore in these parts.

"Twenty-two, and I'm Katie." She stretched a tolerant smile. "Sally was two nights ago. Sally and Jen, I believe. It was me and Cassandra last night."

Prophet pushed himself onto an elbow. His arm was in a sling that Doc Barnhardt had furnished when Prophet dropped off the bodies. The doctor had also offered to furnish laudanum for the pain, but Prophet had declined. He hadn't thought he'd need it, with all the whiskey he'd intended to drink. And he'd been right.

"You mean, I been here two days already?"

Katie was looking around the floor, in the mess of her clothes and his, for some article of her own attire. "That's right, lover." She giggled. "Boy, you do like to have a good time, don't you?"

"I reckon," Prophet sighed, glancing at the washstand, on which two empty whiskey bottles and several beer bottles stood. He was sure there were several more bottles scattered here and there about the floor. "I didn't get into any trouble, did I?"

His heart quickened a little, and he felt a touch of dread. He knew he couldn't have gotten into anything too deep, because he wasn't in jail, an occurrence that was happening less and less as he matured. He was grateful for that, but it was only last year he'd bet a thousand dollars he hadn't had in a poker game, and had gotten into a brawl with a half-breed bean-eater named Oscar Sanchez who'd cracked six of his ribs and chipped two of his teeth. Tracking fugitives to pay off the thousand-dollar debt, when you had to ride hard with six broken ribs, had taught him a healthy fear of his own excess.

Katie had found her camisole and pantaloons and was sitting down in a chair against the wall. She shook the camisole out before her and dropped it over her head, covering those lovely breasts. "Well, that depends on what you call trouble. You drank about six bottles of rye in the last two days, and about twenty bottles of beer, lost about three hundred dollars playing poker with Crazy Jack Thompson, and diddled four whores . . . on credit."

"Well, if that's all," Prophet said, falling back with a relieved sigh, "I'm makin' progress!"

Katie ceased dressing to frown at a broken nail. "You been like this all your life, Lou?"

"How's that?"

She shrugged. "Livin' for fun and money."

He pursed his lips and gazed at the drawn shade, behind which flies buzzed against the fly-flecked window. "I was in the war, Katie. Wore butternut gray. I saw Chattanooga and Utoy Creek, among others." He paused, remembering it against his will—the human viscera, the smell of exposed bowels and blood mixed with burnt powder, grass and trees, the gleam of bone and dead eyes in the bright sun, the buzz of the flies, the pink water of the Tennessee.

Suppressing it, he turned to the girl, forcing a grim smile. "No . . . after that I made a pact with the Devil. I told him that if he showed me one hell of a good time for the rest of the life I had left, I'd shovel all the coal he wanted down below."

She was staring at him, her brown eyes serious, chiding. "That's an awful thing, Lou Prophet . . . makin' a pact like that with the Devil."

"Oh, it ain't that awful," Prophet said, wanting to lighten his own mood as well as hers. "Besides, like I said, I been makin' progress." He grinned big.

She returned it and resumed dressing. "Well . . . don't forget, Mr. Progress, that you owe Cassandra, Sally, Jen, and me each twenty-five dollars." She slipped into the pantaloons and turned to him quickly, remembering something else. "Oh—you owe Jen for a shoe, too."

"A shoe?"

"You broke the heel on one o' hers."

"How'd I do that?"

Katie shrugged. She picked up her remaining clothes, approached the bed, leaned down, and kissed him on the lips. "Don't ask me, lover." She patted his face. "Lordy, you're a handsome devil . . . in a crazy sort o' way."

"What's that mean?"

"Means you're the kinda man I married . . . twice. So don't you think you can charm me with those big green eyes of yours, neither, or that big stick you got between your legs, 'cause you can't." She walked to the door, and turned around with a coquettish flair. "But I'll be glad to haul your ashes whenever you're in town, Lou." She blew him a kiss, opened the door, and left.

He listened to her feet padding down the hall, then down the stairs toward her own room. Quiet followed, with the soft snores of a drunk sleeping off a hangover somewhere down the hall, and ungreased wagon wheels screeching outside, a dog barking, a man calling to another and laughing. Prophet listened hard, trying to suppress the screams of the dying that were always there, like a low inner hum, just beneath his consciousness.

He sighed, reached for his watch, and opened the old turnip. Eleven-thirty. Jesus Christ, had he slept! But then, he supposed he hadn't gotten to sleep until five or six . . . not with the poker game he was beginning to remember, and the two lovely whores riding his bones.

Thinking of the whores made him think of the show-girl. What was her name again? Diamond. Lola Diamond.

"Sounds right falutin." He smiled in spite of his aching, foggy head—remanent of all the booze.

He considered getting up and going downstairs for a bath, then decided he'd lie here a few more minutes and figure out how he was going to approach this woman . . . this Lola Diamond. What would he do if she got nasty? What would he do if this Lola Diamond refused to accompany him down to Johnson City?

Well, by god, he had a job to do and a favor to return. And he'd been paid to boot. He'd throw the cuffs on her. The shackles, too, if he had to.

Prophet reached over to the night table, opened a drawer, and retrieved the show poster he'd placed there, after swiping it off the wall at Dave's Place. It was a circular advertising Big Dan Walthrop's Traveling Dolls and Roadhouse Show, giving the names of the four "dolls" and telling where they were going to be and when. Typical roadhouse fair. Prophet had learned from Dave himself that the troupe master stood at least six-five and weighed a good two-fifty.

"That's all right," Prophet told himself. "Guys like him's what the Peacemaker was invented for."

Reluctant to start a day of business when it seemed he'd only just started having fun, he tossed the covers back, crawled out of bed, and started gathering his clothes. Dressed, he went downstairs to the dining room and ordered a steak-and-egg breakfast complete with a tall glass of milk and a cup of hot, black coffee with a medicinal jigger of rye whiskey.

When he'd finished his food, he drank two more cups of laced coffee, lingering over a cigarette, then paid his bill and went out. Stepping onto the boardwalk, he watched two whiskey drummers cross the street in front of Dave's Place, holding their crisp bowlers on their heads. Both men wore broadcloth suits and vests, gold watch chains bouncing at their sides.

The civilized attire of the two men made Prophet conscious of his own shabby dress—worn, undershot boots, faded denims with threadbare knees, a calico shirt that reeked of stale smoke and sour whiskey, and a ratty Stetson beaten by hail, wind, and snow, and sweat-stained the color of old burlap. Half-consciously seeing himself through the eyes of Miss Diamond, he wrinkled his nose.

"I look like hell."

He turned and made a beeline for Sandoval's Drygoods. The bell jingled as he pushed through the door.

A short, stout Mexican with a wispy black mustache and wearing a white apron looked up from dusting a display of women's soaps.

Prophet stopped in the shadows just inside the door. "Paco," he called, "can you set me up in a new suit for thirty bucks?"

Paco frowned. "Thirty bucks?"

"That's all I got. I'll be needin' boots, as well."

The frown still in place, Paco said, "What you want a suit for, Lou—you're a *bounty* hunter." The man's frown was instantly replaced by a grin, his small, white teeth gleaming in the light angling through the windows on his right.

Unable to see the humor in his request, Prophet snapped, "Can you do it or do I take my business elsewhere?"

The man shrugged exaggeratedly. "Okay, okay. I feex you up, Lou."

He beckoned Prophet to a back wall, where men's clothes were displayed on wood shelves and hanging from racks. Hemming and hawing aloud, he measured Prophet with his gaze, then produced a pair of whipcord trousers from one of the shelves, and a wool vest and frock coat from a rack. Placing it all on a straight-backed chair before a floor mirror, he retrieved a neatly folded and pinned shirt from a wire bin.

"That the best you can do?" Prophet said, gazing critically at the shirt.

"For thirty bucks?" Paco asked, incredulous.

"What about that one?" Prophet said, pointing at another shirt hanging from a display rack behind the coats and vests.

"That's linen."

"How much?"

"Twelve-feefty."

Prophet aimed a sharp look at the proprietor. "My credit's good here, ain't it?"

Paco was incensed. "For *twelve-feefty*?"

"Come on, Paco, throw it in. Remember how I covered for you with Estelle when she thought you were diddling that whore back in the pens . . . and she was right? Huh? You remember that?"

Paco whipped his head around, red growing beneath the almond of his cheeks. "Shhh! She's in the back room!"

"Throw it in."

"Okay—it's in, it's in."

Another dickering war broke out when it came to the calfskin boots, which were fifty dollars and ran Prophet's bill up to an even hundred. The war ended quickly, however, when Estelle walked out of the back room to wait on two other ladies looking for muslin.

"Okay, okay," Paco said, quickly lowering his voice, "I throw in the boots! Calfskin . . . *madre* Maria . . ."

An hour later, Prophet walked out of Haugen's Tonsorial Parlor, looking just like what he was—a big, sunburned, freshly shaved and bathed bounty hunter stuffed into a suit complete with a brown felt bowler that would have been the envy of any whiskey drummer in Montana Territory, and a pair of calfskin boots so soft they felt like moccasins.

The new duds gave him confidence, however. They made him feel downright civilized and the most respectable thing to hit the West since the railroad. He'd always wondered what wearing a suit would feel like, and now he knew. It made you feel like sticking your nose up and your chest out and not being quite so friendly to folks.

He thought he suddenly understood all the businessmen he'd known and disliked.

Now all he needed was a badge to pin to his vest. It

would lend him an official air, and he thought it necessary to approach Miss Diamond looking official. It wasn't
that he wanted to impress her. Well, that wasn't his sole
purpose, anyway. The badge would lend him a bureau-
cratic respectability, making it a hell of a lot easier for
him to get her on the stage. Yessir, the badge and the
pickup order would make a package not even a jaded
showgirl could refuse. Once he got her to Johnson City,
he'd tell her he wasn't a lawman.

Well, the only place to find a badge was a sheriff's
office. With a fateful sigh, he stepped off the boardwalk
and headed across the dusty street, his new boots
squawking like a baby duck on his heels. Midway, he
met a gent who looked a lot like him—big and sunburned
and hard-looking—but without the friendly glitter in
Prophet's eyes. Besides that, the man had an enormous
nose—a nose so large it made Prophet's look small.

Prophet tipped his head to the man. The man tipped
back. They passed with no further ado. But when the
other man came to the boardwalk Prophet had just left,
he turned to watch Prophet approach the sheriff's office
and knock on the splintery door. The man swept the folds
of his claw-hammer coat back from a brace of well-oiled
forty-fours, and watched with faintly smirking interest as
Prophet stepped inside the jail and closed the door behind
him.

The man watched the closed door thoughtfully, rubbing his tongue over his teeth. Then a knowing light entered his gaze, and he headed out in search of a whiskey
and a cool place to wait.

4

MARGARET JANE OLSON, a.k.a. Lola Diamond, sat in the driver's box of the wagon on whose cover the words "BIG DAN WALTHROP'S TRAVELING DOLLS AND ROADHOUSE SHOW" had been written in large block letters. She wore a floppy-brimmed straw hat and the clinging, low-cut green dress of cheap material she always wore traveling between show stops. But in an effort to look as nice as she could without sacrificing expensive cloth to the ravages of the sun, wind, and dust of the trail, she wore about her slender neck a choker with a single pearl, and tiny pearl earrings.

You never knew who you might meet on this godforsaken prairie; she'd once met a Russian prince, of all people, in Dakota, of all places. He had been amazed at her hair, which he had described as red as a Western sunset, which it was, she was proud to admit. It contrasted the sky blue of her eyes and the porcelain cream of her skin to bewitching effect. Her full lips, which she painted the same shade of red as her hair, made an exquisite, pouting O beneath her delicate nose.

Now she pulled the brim of her hat down lower, protecting her face from the sun, and scowled as she rode with the reins of the two-horse team lightly in her gloved hands. Lola Diamond, as she preferred to be called these days, was not happy. Not only was she once again traversing the freight roads and army trails of the middle of nowhere, crooning and dancing every night for drunk miners, gandy dancers, cowpokes, freighters, and outlaws in every tumbleweed town and stage stop in southern Montana, she was having to drive a wagon while "Big Dan" snored off a hangover in the box behind her.

How in the world had she ended up here? she wondered, casting a look about the sunbaked plain rolling off in every direction, relieved by knolls and ridges, occasional buffalo wallows and brush-lined water courses. Here and there a rock shelf jutted up, scaly with ancient sandstone, and the far western horizon was a toothy, dark blue line of mountains—no doubt another godforsaken range in which some backwater mining town sat, or a roadhouse, and where Big Dan would have her and the other girls playing tomorrow night or the night after or the night after that.

Big Dan seemed to love these forlorn, off-the-beaten-path places. He'd no doubt run up against the law somewhere in his seedy past, and didn't want to be seen anywhere he might be recognized. Lola preferred places a little more hopping, where there was more of a chance some agent from a big-city playhouse might discover her and give her a chance to achieve the kind of fame she'd not only been born for, but worked hard at attaining practically her entire life.

She'd been born in Utica, New York, to a mild-

mannered, unambitious father and an ambitious, hard-
working mother who ran a boardinghouse and who gave
her beautiful, precocious Margaret Jane acting lessons by
accomplished East Coast thespians. When Margaret Jane
was twelve, her mother sold her boardinghouse, and she,
Margaret Jane, and the reluctant father hopped the Union
Pacific to take advantage of the acting and singing op-
portunities offered by the burgeoning seaport of San
Francisco.

Only Margaret Jane and her mother made it to California, however, the father having fallen ill and dying
during a layover in Kelton, Utah. Not to be thwarted, the
stalwart Olson women journeyed on to San Francisco,
where Mrs. Olson secured for Margaret Jane singing and
dancing stints galore, but only in perilous bars and taverns along the waterfront. No jobs were available in the
more respectable theaters, which, the Olsons were exas-
perated to learn, had been monopolized by a few local
families with connections, one of which was the Booth
family, made infamous by Edward's assassination of
President Lincoln.

Compounding young Margaret Jane's problems, her
mother died of food poisoning, leaving Margaret Jane,
then sixteen, utterly alone. What saved her from the hor-
rors that befell most young women alone and down and
out in San Francisco was an older actress and singer
named Naomi Tate, who invited Margaret Jane to accompany her and her traveling theatrical troupe to the wild
and woolly—but highly profitable—mining camps in the
northern territories.

Things went well in that rough country populated by
cowboys, Indians, miners, and outlaws, and the playbills
identified Margaret Jane as "Amber Skye"—the stage
name had been Naomi's idea—until the troupe headed
back to San Francisco. Liking the wild and woolly West,

making good money there, and believing it was there she would one day be discovered by the right talent scout, Margaret Jane joined one traveling show after another, playing in places like Virginia City, Johnson City, Medicine Bow, Billings, and Bannack—and every roadhouse and stage stop in between.

It was in Johnson City that she ran into the trouble that landed her in the Beaverhead country. She remembered it all now as she squinted off across the sun-scorched plain, the sharp smell of sage bringing tears to her eyes. At least she thought it was the sage. Maybe it was the memory of that horrible night back in Johnson City, after she'd gotten through her usual string of numbers at the Stockmen's Hotel, had gone to bed, then gotten up for water and heard the trouble in Hoyt Farley's office. . . .

No. She didn't want to think of that now. It was too terrifying a memory. She, Lola Diamond, as she'd been known since her last night in Johnson City, had to keep her head up and stick to the back country where, hopefully, no one would recognize her. In a few months she'd make enough money working for Big Dan that she could book passage back to Denver or San Francisco, where certainly her considerable experience would secure her a job . . . somewhere.

And where no one from Johnson City would ever find her. . . .

As the big wheels of the wagon rolled along, the horses's hooves thumping on the well-churned trail, kicking up the alkali dust like flour, the snores behind Lola suddenly ceased. A moment later Big Dan stuck his head through the white canvas cover. He blinked his eyes and smacked his lips as he crawled onto the seat beside Lola.

"See any Indians?" he asked.

Lola jerked him a startled look. "Indians?"

Big Dan chuckled deeply. "Guess not. That's good."

"You said the Indians were peaceful in these parts," Lola reminded the big, red-bearded man.

He was twisting the upswept ends of his mustache, badly in need of trimming. With his idiotically protruding eyes, scarred nose, and huge, ungainly frame, he looked more like a bouncer in some Leadville saloon than the master of a road show. But then a bouncer in a Leadville saloon was exactly what he'd been two years ago, before he'd inherited the wagons, costumes, and horses from his cousin, the former owner, who'd died from a knife wound during a saloon brawl.

Only one of the show's original actresses had remained with the show, but it wasn't hard recruiting actors and singers in these parts, where everyone but the miners seemed dissatisfied with his or her current occupation, and was desperate for money. For Lola, who had met Big Dan only a month ago, it had been either sign up with the man, who'd been pulling out for the Beaverhead country the next day, or get her throat slashed and her body thrown to the dogs at the Johnson City dump.

Big Dan pulled a flask from an inside pocket of his frock coat. Lined with red satin, it was another trophy he'd inherited from his cousin, and about two sizes too small. Big Dan's round shoulders strained the seams, and the cuffs stopped well short of his wrists. "Mostly the Injuns are right peaceful around here, but you never know. The Bannacks are raisin' hell over Utah-way, so you never know what the Blackfeet and Crows are gonna try pullin'. Sometimes one tribe gets a hell-raisin' idea from another. . . ." He shrugged, uncorked the flask, and raised it to his lips.

Lola's cheeks flushed with anger. She scrutinized the man with narrow-eyed disdain. "You might have told me that before you decided to nod off."

Big Dan took another slug from the flask, smacked his

lips, and recorked the bottle. "Sorry . . . I wasn't feelin' too good." He gave Lola a sidelong glance, grinning wolfishly and stealing another of many looks down her dress.

"Well, you seem to be feeling fine now. Here"—she tossed him the reins—"you can have your job back."

Dan chuckled and returned the flask to his coat. Taking up the reins, he grinned. "You sure are pretty, Lola. You're the prettiest girl in my troupe. I sure wish you'd give me a poke."

Accustomed to his crude advances, she merely rolled her eyes. "If wishes were horses, Dan . . ."

He grinned through his beard. "Never know—might be fun."

Lola sighed and looked off. Here she was, miles from civilization with this tawdry troupe of underpaid actresses and this moron, who didn't know Shakespeare from vaudeville and who accosted her with his goatish hunger every chance he got.

Holding the reins at his chest, Dan nudged Lola with his elbow and winked. "I didn't say I'd pay ya for it, Lola." He guffawed. "If I don't pay, it ain't whorin'—now, ain't that right? Haw, haw, haw!"

She gave a long, tired sigh and turned to the man showing his long horse teeth under his mustache as he grinned, pleased with himself. "When are we gonna stop? I got nature to tend, and I bet the other girls do, too. Looks to me there's a creek right over there."

Big Dan pulled a watch from his pocket and flipped the lid. "Well, it's already one o'clock. I'd like to make Henry's Crossing by three. It's gonna take us a while to set up, an' I know you girls are gonna wanna have naps and baths like ya always do. . . ."

Anger flashed in Lola's eyes as she turned sideways to face the big man. "Listen, you scoundrel—I drove this wagon all morning while you slept off your hangover.

Now you stop so we can pee and the horses can drink, goddamn you!"

"All right, all right!" Big Dan relented, swinging the horses toward the creek. When they approached the cut-bank, he said, "You got a half hour. No more, an' that's final. These wagons are pullin' out at two-thirty."

Lola hardly heard the last two sentences, for she'd jumped down from the wagon before the horses had halted, and was walking back along the trail as the other two wagons approached, driven by two other actresses—Minnie Calhoun and Glyneen Night. All the actresses took turns driving the second wagon. When they weren't driving, they usually slept in the wagons or looked over song sheets or playbooks, or sewed costumes.

"Mr. Big-Shot's givin' us a nature break, girls," Lola called. "Pull up yonder."

She beckoned as she turned and started down the shallow bank, heading for a stand of cottonwoods in a wide horseshoe of the creek, about a hundred yards away. The other actresses climbed down from their wagons. The two younger girls, Glyneen Night and Audrey Fare, still had enough energy after the arduous journey from the last gold camp to jostle each other and laugh as they approached the cottonwoods. Lola was only twenty-one, still young by most standards, but in the last month or so she'd felt old. Old and angry and tired.

She pulled up her dress, dropped her bloomers, and squatted behind a cottonwood. Audrey Fare rustled the grass as she approached and squatted behind a tree only ten yards to Lola's right. Audrey was only a year younger than Lola, but because of Lola's superior beauty, talent, and mysterious past, Audrey looked up to her, in much the same way Lola had once looked up to the dynamic, worldly Naomi Tate.

"Lola," the girl said as she peed. "Can I ask you a question?"

"As long as it's not personal," Lola snapped.

She'd made it clear after she'd joined the troupe that she would entertain no questions regarding her immediate circumstances; no questions regarding what she was obviously running from back in Johnson City. Naturally the others, including Big Dan, were curious, since Big Dan had hired her in the middle of the night and she'd abruptly appeared the next morning as the wagons were heading out of town.

"Oh, it's not about you, Lola," the girl said mournfully. "It's about me. Do you think Harvey'll stay true?"

"Harvey?"

"You know—the gent I met in Lofton?"

Snickers rose from a tree behind Lola.

Lola turned angrily. "Minnie, you hush your mouth!" To Audrey, she said regretfully. "Honey, how long did you know the man?"

For several seconds there was only the sound of the prairie breeze churning the cottonwood leaves high above their heads. Cloud shadows swept the gurgling creek and the clover, mustard, and foxtails along its banks.

"Two nights," Audrey said. She stood holding her dress above her waist as she adjusted her bloomers.

"Did you allow him to . . . well . . . you know . . . ?"

Audrey shrugged passively. "Well . . . yeah. . . ."

Minnie snickered again behind the other tree.

"Did he promise himself to you before or after you gave yourself?" Lola asked Audrey.

More snickers, louder this time.

"Minnie, I don't want to have to tell you again!" Lola cried. The snickers ceased.

"Before," Audrey said thinly.

Lola got her bloomers in place, smoothed her dress

down over her legs, and walked over to Audrey, who stood holding herself before the cottonwood. Her thin blond hair blew about her face.

"Well, I'm not going to sugarcoat it for you, sweetie," Lola said, taking one of the girl's hands in hers. "But any man who promises himself to you after he's known you only a night or two is either a jasper or a pecker-wood—a varmint of the lowest kind. A snake in the tall grass. Most likely, he promised himself just so he could get in your drawers. Now that he got what he wanted, he's no doubt promised himself to two or three other girls since we left Lofton."

"Oh, Lola, he wouldn't!" the girl cried.

Lola put her arms around her. She knew what it was like to be hurt by a man. It had happened to her once, when she was only sixteen. You grow up fast in this business. She knew one thing, though—she'd never let it happen again.

"Oh, yes, he would," she said, rocking the girl gently back and forth in her arms. "It'll take you a while, but eventually you'll learn how to tell the snakes from those men who'll walk the straight and narrow with a girl."

Audrey lifted her head to look into Lola's eyes. "You find any of those men yet, Lola?"

Lola looked away, frowning. "No," she said at length. "No . . . for all my talkin', I haven't found any man like that myself." She held the girl for a while longer, then she pushed her away and smiled. "But I'll tell you as soon as I find more than one, and you can have first pick of the pack. How's that?"

Audrey smiled through a sob, and nodded her head.

"In the meantime, I think I hear a snake right now," Lola said.

Audrey frowned. "Huh?"

"Wait." Lola bent down, lifted the hem of her dress,

and removed a small, silver-plated pistol from a sheath strapped to her calf. Turning, she swung the pistol around toward a stand of high grass and chokecherry shrubs, and squeezed off a round. The gun cracked sharply, spitting smoke and fire.

"Wait!" erupted a man's voice from the brush. "Wait, goddamnit, Lola! It's me!"

"I know it's you!" Lola returned. "It's you trying to get a peek at four women tending nature, you pathetic son of a bitch."

There was a thrashing in the weeds, and a bush moved, but Big Dan did not show himself. "Don't shoot!"

Lola had a mind to go ahead and plug the dirty bastard, but then where would she be? She could take over the troupe herself. If anyone asked about Big Dan, she could say he'd gotten overly randy one night—which wouldn't be a lie, the way he was always pawing the other girls, and had even talked Minnie and Glyneen into sleeping with him for special favors—and she'd plugged him. The other girls would probably even corroborate her story.

The only problem was four women without a man were sitting ducks out here, for anything that happened along. They certainly couldn't ride into the mining camps they played every night without a man riding shotgun. Big Dan was worthless most ways, but he was a big son of a bitch, and he wielded a shotgun well.

Lola lowered the gun to her side. "Get back to the wagon and do your job for a change. You ever try that again, you bastard, I'll shoot you between the eyes."

"Okay, Lola, okay," Dan said, snapping twigs and rustling branches as he made his way out of the bushes, his hands raised to his chest. "I was just havin' fun, Lola." He grinned. "Don't take it so serious. The others don't— right, Glyneen?"

The other girls had gathered around Lola when they'd

heard the gunshot. Now Big Dan, grinning like a naughty schoolboy, draped an arm around Glyneen and Minnie as he made his way back toward the wagons. "You two know how I am, don't you? Big Dan just likes to have fun. . . ." He went on talking as he walked with Glyneen and Minnie on either side of him, giving truckling, inaudible answers to his pandering questions.

Lola turned to Audrey, who smiled devilishly. "Would you really have shot him?"

"Right through the eyes," Lola said.

She turned to stare across the creek and the bending weeds rising on the other side to a low sandstone ridge. Everything was made so terribly small by the sky that Lola wanted to cry. Her mother was dead, and here she was toting a pistol on her leg and fending off randy troupe masters in Indian country.

Where were the silk top hats and leather buggies, ladies decked out in crinoline and lace? The thirty-dollar rooms and the caviar? Where were the big shows with her name in large, fancy letters, the bejeweled social circles in which her mother had wanted her so desperately to romp?

"Come on, Lola," Audrey urged, tugging on her sleeve. "We'd best get back to the wagons. It's on—"

"Yes, I know," Lola sighed, unwillingly emerging from her reverie. "It's on to Henry's Crossing."

She brushed her sweat-damp hair back from her face and started toward the wagons. Could her life get any worse?

5

"WELL . . . LOOK AT you!" Sheriff Fitzsimmons exclaimed, looking up from his newspaper as Lou Prophet entered his office. "Good Lord, man—what you got going now?"

Prophet flushed, embarrassed, and looked down at his new duds. True, he might've overdone it, but he knew that, for women, first impressions were key. While he wasn't trying to seduce Miss Diamond in the customary sense, he was in a way.

He shrugged. His tooled black boots squeaked as he lifted onto the balls of his feet. "Just decided it was time I cleaned up a little, is all."

The sheriff worked his nostrils as he sniffed the air. "What's that smell? That you, too?"

"Just had a shave and a haircut," Prophet said, rubbing his clean jaw. "Told the barber to give me the works."

"Well, that he did, all right. If you don't leave soon

it's going to take me a good month to air the place out."
Fitzsimmons grinned, pleased with the joke. The grin
broke into a deep-chested chuckle as the gray-haired little
man leaned back in his chair and laced his fingers over
his belly. "Oh, I see."

"What?"

"This is for that showgirl, that Lola Diamond."

Prophet played dumb. He knew Fitz wouldn't understand—not at his age, not at *any* age. "What do you
mean?"

"These new duds and the haircut and that smelly
water—that's so you'll make a good impression on her.
You're gonna try to court her while you're takin' her
back to Johnson City—see if you can't get a little more
out of the ride than a hundred and fifty greenbacks." Fitzsimmons winked and nodded his head, washed-out eyes
flashing.

"That ain't it at all, Sheriff," Prophet said. He sat down
in the chair before the old man's battered desk. "This is
just my way of trying to make the woman feel at ease.
If I approach her dressed like I usually am—well, hell,
she'll probably turn tail and run. And her boss'll probably
pull a gun and fill my ass with buckshot."

Fitzsimmons squinted his eyes skeptically. "So this is
just to charm her, you mean—so you can get her on the
stage without any fuss?"

"Exactly." But Prophet began to wonder if that were
entirely true. He did have a soft spot for good-looking
women, and if this girl was a showgirl, she had to be
attractive.

Fitzsimmons's face reddened, his nostrils swelling.
"Yeah, I believe that just like I believe all your other
cockamamy horse hocky. Now tell me what the hell
you're doin' here, so I can get rid of you and your
stench."

Prophet flicked a speck of dust off the arm of his new coat and said offhandedly, "Just wanted to say adios, Sheriff, and see if McCreedy sent anything else while I was . . . enjoying myself." He frowned, shifting his gaze to the door behind the sheriff.

Noticing the sudden change of expression, Fitzsimmons turned, his swivel chair squeaking as he shot a look behind him and said, "What . . . what the hell you lookin' at?"

"You got somebody back in the cell block?"

"Huh? Yeah . . . I got a kid some drovers brought in two days ago . . . a horse thief waitin' on the circuit judge." Fitzsimmons turned back to Prophet, his downy eyebrows knit. "Why?"

"I thought I heard something . . . a diggin' sound."

"A diggin' sound?" The sheriff turned back to the door and paused, listening. To Prophet, he said, "I don't hear nothin'."

Prophet shrugged. "Must just be my ears goin' bad. Never mind. Anyway—"

"Now just a minute, goddamnit!" the sheriff said angrily, waving Prophet silent. "I better check it out." He produced a ring of keys from a desk drawer, climbed out of his chair, and disappeared through the cell block door.

Immediately, Prophet rose from his seat, swung around the desk, and started opening and closing drawers. He stopped when he found what he was looking for—a five-pointed deputy sheriff's star. He pocketed the badge, shut the drawer, and quickly returned to his seat just as Fitzsimmons reappeared.

"I'll say you're hearin' things," the sheriff grouched as he moved toward the desk. "The kid's dead asleep back there."

"I could have swore I heard diggin' sounds," Prophet said with a shrug. "Must've been all that shootin' in the cabin. My ears still feel like they're full of cotton."

"Well, they're full of somethin'." Fitzsimmons opened a desk drawer, tossed the keys inside, and slammed it. Sitting back down with a grunt and a curse, he said, "Now what'd you say you're doin' here?"

"Just sayin' good-bye," Prophet said, standing and heading for the door.

Fitzsimmons watched him suspiciously, chewing his mustache. "Bye? You came to tell me *bye*?"

"That's all, Fitz."

"That's *Sheriff* Fitz*simmons* to you, Prophet!" The red-faced badge-toter paused to scrutinize the bounty hunter with befuddled disdain, the muscles at his jaw hinges twitching for all they were worth. "What the hell are you up to?"

" 'Bout six-three," Prophet quipped, stepping out the door. "See ya, Sheriff."

"Not if I see you first, Prophet," Fitzsimmons yelled. "And you be careful you don't hurt that girl. Remember, she ain't no prisoner . . . she's a *witness*!"

"I'll remember that," Prophet said.

"And for godsakes, leave the door open!"

Leaving the office door standing wide behind him, Prophet headed across the street, hoping to be safely out of town before Fitzsimmons discovered the badge missing from his drawer. Prophet hadn't asked for the badge because he knew Fitzsimmons wouldn't have given him one. To wear a sheriff's star, you had to be deputized, and Fitzsimmons was more likely to deputize one of the girls at the Queen Bee than Lou Prophet.

Walking quickly, the bounty hunter went back to the hotel, retrieved his gear, and paid his bill. He delivered his rifle, shotgun, and saddlebags to the stage office. He didn't want to be carrying anything but the subpoena when he approached the girl. That accomplished, he went over to Dave's Place and ordered a beer from the scowling, cadaverous bartender who was trying to get a new keg primed as he snapped at his ten-year-old helper.

Prophet paid his nickel and headed for a table not far from the big plate-glass window. He noticed another man sitting nearby—the tall, hard-looking gent with the hub-sized nose he'd passed on the street when he'd been heading for the sheriff's office. He'd noticed the man first because of his nose, then because the man was wearing a suit, and, being in the suit frame of mind, Prophet had given it a quick appraisal. As he had, he'd noticed the two Remingtons tied low on the man's thighs—a fancy brace of forty-fours in hand-tooled holsters.

The man was obviously a gunslick, but gunslicks were not out of place in Henry's Crossing, one of the wilder towns on the northern frontier. You got all kinds coming through here, with the river trade being what it was, and with the mining country all around. Not to mention the cattle herds moving in. Not long ago Prophet had ear-marked Henry's Crossing as the next Abilene—not a nice place to raise a family by any estimation, but a profitable haunt for a man of Prophet's profession.

He didn't pay the gunslick more than passing attention. Sitting down with his beer, he slumped back in his chair and watched the busy street beyond the window, where a steady flow of freight wagons kicked up dust and dropped it thick on the shipping crates, kegs, and mining equipment that lined the ferry docks, waiting for the big mule wagons that would haul it to every saloon and mercantile within a hundred square miles. One team after another rocked and rattled by, the curses of the skinners rising on the warm April air. Men laughed and cajoled, horses whinnied, dogs barked, chickens clucked, and the cottonwoods along the wide, green river churned their silver-edged leaves.

Watching and drinking, Prophet waited for the traveling theatrical troupe, which would no doubt pass before this very window, and thought about how he was going to get Miss Lola Diamond separated from her troupe and on the stage, which was due to leave at five-thirty this afternoon. He hoped she made it by then. Since her show started at seven, he thought she would. If not, he'd have to wait for the next stagecoach, two days hence. Leaving that late would make it tough to get into Johnson City on time. Remembering the urgent tone of Owen McCreedy's letter, Prophet watched the traffic with growing anxiety.

It was nearly four-thirty when Big Dan's Traveling Dolls and Roadhouse Show rolled past the saloon from the east, the covered wagons separated by about thirty dusty feet, the ungreased wheel hubs squawking like geese. Prophet exhaled a long, relieved breath and tipped back the last of his third beer. Standing, he donned his hat, walked outside, and headed for the Waddy's Cottage.

The troupe had pulled up before the hotel, and the women and one man were climbing tiredly down from the wagons, dusting themselves off.

Prophet knew that nabbing the girl now, exhausted after a long wagon ride, wasn't the kindest way of accomplishing his task. But considering the time constraint, what else could he do? What worried him, however, was Big Dan. As Prophet approached the wagons, he could see the troupe master was easily as big as he'd been described.

"You girls go on in and have your baths and naps and whatnot," Big Dan said now, as the women gathered on the boardwalk, slapping the trail dust from their dresses and flexing their tired muscles. "I'll carry the trunks up as soon as I—"

"Yeah, I know—as soon as you've had about seventeen beers," one of the girls finished for him.

Big Dan made no reply; he was in too big a hurry to get over to Dave's Place, eyes wide with the image of a frothy beer in his fist. He was so distracted that he didn't even glance at Prophet, who politely tipped his hat as the troupe master thundered past on the boardwalk, big boots fanning up dust with every heavy-footed step.

Prophet paused, his back to the mercantile, and watched Big Dan walk away behind him and turn into the saloon. Prophet was pleased by how things were panning out. With Big Dan cutting the trail dust in Dave's, it shouldn't be too difficult to nab the girl. Thinking it over and liking the idea better and better, the bounty hunter reached into his coat pocket for the deputy sheriff's star and pinned it to his wool vest, making sure it was hid by the left lapel of his new coat. He didn't want to reveal it until he had to. Enough people around town knew his true identity to muck things up good and plumb if they spied the badge.

He turned back to the wagons. Three of the girls had gathered around the back of the last wagon. The fourth was inside, handing down carpetbags to the others.

"Ladies, let me help you with those," Prophet said as he approached the group.

"Thanks, mister," one of them said.

"Yeah, thanks," said another.

"No problem at all," Prophet said, taking a bag from the girl inside the wagon.

He looked at her and almost recoiled from her beauty—the oval-shaped, elegant face with a narrow, decisive nose and widely spaced blue eyes. She was in her early twenties, a stunning beauty whose green dress clung to her kindly, accentuating the fullness of her breasts and the slenderness of her waist. What really caught Prophet's attention was her hair, which was the deep umber of hot coals as a raging fire burned down to cinders. It brushed her slender neck in curly waves.

"Much obliged," she said with an understated smile, lifting her eyes to regard him guardedly from under the brim of her floppy straw hat. The hat gave her the air of a tomboy. A tomboy, that was, with full, pursed lips and skin as smooth as water.

"Uh . . . no problem at all," he said, his heart thumping as he recognized Lola Diamond. The sheriff's description of her had not done her justice, and Prophet was glad he'd had the good sense to buy new duds. She indeed appeared to be a woman who'd judge a man by his attire. "You must be Miss Diamond."

"That's right," she said, frowning curiously, stepping onto the wagon's end gate. He took her slender arm and helped her down as she asked, "And you are . . . ?"

"Louis B. Prophet at your service, ma'am," Prophet announced with his best Southern gentleman's smile. "I'm in the whiskey trade."

"Whiskey drummer?"

"Oh, don't worry—I'm not here to sell you whiskey, ma'am. I'm a big fan of yours, and when I saw your wagons pass by the saloon yonder . . . well . . . I just thought I'd see if I could help you ladies with your bags."

He exaggerated his Georgia accent, which he'd found to have a soothing effect on women. He smiled disarmingly, lifted the crisp bowler, then set it gently down on his head and glanced behind him to make sure Sheriff Fitzsimmons wasn't within hearing range. The inimical sheriff would no doubt have gotten quite a laugh from Prophet's performance, and probably have foiled the whole thing.

"Thanks anyway," the girl said with a polite smile, "but we'll carry our own bags." A cautious one, she. One so lovely would have to be.

"Oh, come on, Lola," one of the other girls dissented. "I say if the kind man wants to carry our bags, we let him."

"Me, too, Lola," another chimed in. "My backs hurts."

"Hey, thanks, mister!" the third girl said before Lola could object.

"No trouble at all, no trouble at all," Prophet sang, hefting all four carpetbags under his arms. "Show me the way, ladies!"

Hauling the carpetbags, Prophet followed the tired, trail-weary women into the hotel, and then waited while they registered. When Lola and one of the others had gotten their room keys, Prophet followed them up the stairs, admiring the way the green dress clung to the redhead's legs, tracing the contours of her shapely thighs as she walked. In spite of the pain that hefting the bags inspired in his shoulder, he was growing more and more fond of his job.

"Much obliged," Lola said dully as she stood in her open doorway. The girl she was sharing a room with had gone in ahead of her. The other two had already gone into the room next door, and had closed the door after effusively thanking Prophet for his help. "I'll tell Dave over at the saloon to draw you a beer on Big Dan," Lola added as she turned away and started closing the door in Prophet's face.

"Well, uh . . ." Prophet sighed. Here it was, the moment of truth. "I'm afraid I won't be hanging around. And I'm afraid . . ." He let the sentence trail off, feeling like a genuine shit heel for what he was about to do. But he had a strong sense that getting her to Johnson City in four days meant a great deal more to Owen McCreedy than what the sheriff had expressed in his note.

Deciding to let the subpoena speak for itself, Prophet

pulled it out of his shirt pocket and handed it over. "Here . . . this is for you."

She frowned. "What's this?" She took the paper, unfolded it, and began reading. Almost instantly, her face paled. Her rich lips parted as she inhaled deeply. She lowered the document to her side and narrowed her eyes at him. "What the hell's a subpoena?"

Silently amused by the girl's salty tongue but caught off-guard by the question, Prophet said, "Well . . . it's a . . . a legally binding document . . . that says . . . well . . . that says you have to accompany me down to Johnson City, to testify at a hearing." Suddenly unsure what a subpoena was himself, and calling on the deputy sheriff's badge for backup, he drew his coat back from the star only long enough for her to glimpse it. He doubted she knew the difference between a deputy sheriff's star and a deputy marshal's badge, but he figured she could read the writing engraved on the tin. "Louis B. Prophet, deputy U.S. marshal. That paper says you have to accompany me to Johnson City. The sheriff there wants to talk to you."

"You're here to *arrest* me?"

"No, ma'am," Prophet said, vehemently shaking his head. "I'm here to *escort* you to Johnson City."

She took several steps back, slapping a hand to her chest. "Well, I won't go. I *can't* go!"

"Miss, I'm sorry—"

Before he could finish the sentence, she slammed the door. Prophet jammed one of his new boots between the door and the frame, halting the door so suddenly it cracked. The girl screamed and threw her weight against it. She was no match for the bounty hunter, who heaved it open with a grunt.

The girl gave up on the door, ran across the room, grabbed a pitcher, and tossed it at Prophet. Heavy with water, it made it only halfway, hitting the floor with a thunderous bang. Dumbfounded, Prophet stared at the water spreading across the floor. He saw the girl hike her leg on a chair and reach inside her dress. Having seen this move before, Prophet lunged for her, grabbed her wrist, and removed the hideout gun—a .32-caliber Hopkins and Allen, an underpowered little snub-nose but reasonably effective at close range—just as she removed it from the sheath strapped to her thigh. She cried angrily, jerking her empty hand from his grasp and falling against the dresser.

Prophet stuck the pea shooter in his cartridge belt, his mind reeling. He hadn't expected a reaction this violent. He'd thought the deputy U.S. marshal guise would sedate her, resign her to the fact she was going to Johnson City whether she wanted to or not. The plan hadn't worked, and he was dumbfounded and perplexed. He had a wild female on his hands, which, he was quickly discovering, was akin to wrestling a wounded bobcat in a Conestoga wagon.

The problem was a dull ache in his brain: How do you restrain a woman without hurting her?

"Listen, miss . . . please . . . I—"

His voice was cut off by the other girl, who jumped to her feet screaming like a banshee.

Prophet turned to her, opening his hands acquiescently. He stopped when he heard thundering footsteps and raised voices behind him. Turning to cover his flank, he was too slow to see Miss Diamond dart forward, hiking her dress above her ankles and lifting her right foot until it had connected soundly with his groin.

Prophet had taken a direct hit in the balls a few times in the past—in his line of work, it was nearly unavoidable—but he couldn't remember any man kicking him this hard.

He doubled over with an enormous groan and a sigh, automatically bringing his hands to his crotch. Giving an angry cry, the girl punched him twice in the head, up-ending his hat and staggering him sideways.

He fell to his knees and glanced up. All four girls were gathering around him—concernedly, defensively, angrily. It didn't take them long to assess his apparent threat to one of their own. One kicked him in the shoulder, another in the ribs. Screaming oaths he'd never heard from female lips, another pulled his hair and socked him in the ear so hard that the entire right side of his head went numb.

Amid the blows from foot and fist, Prophet tried gaining his feet. Before he could do so, he heard boots thump into the room, the floorboards complaining above the din of the admonishing women. Turning and lifting his head slightly, he saw the man with the big nose standing just inside the door, outside of which three or four other hotel guests had gathered, looking shocked and confused.

The man was aiming one of his fancy pistols at the girls. His mouth was a dark slash across his face, and his heavy brows were knit, but there was a humorous flash in his eyes. One at a time, the girls saw him. They fell instantly silent, mouths agape, eyes sliding between the gun and the gaze of the man wielding it.

When the room had quieted, the man said to Prophet reasonably, "I was just walkin' by when I heard the commotion . . . uh . . . Marshal. Looks like you need a little help."

Still clutching his bruised balls, which felt as though they'd swollen to twice their normal size, Prophet gave a grunt and a feeble nod. Blood trickled from his cut lip. He flushed, embarrassed. "Obliged."

"Which one you after . . . or all of 'em?"

"Just this one here."

Lola's eyes darted to Prophet. Clenching her teeth stubbornly, she shook her head. "I will not go with you."

Someone from the doorway cleared his throat. "You . . . you want I should call the sheriff?" a man's thin voice inquired.

The well-dressed, big-nosed man half-turned to the doorway. "I don't think that'll be necessary," he said. "This man here's a deputy U.S. marshal. He was trying to arrest one of the girls when they all attacked him . . . the poor son of a bitch." The man addressed Prophet pityingly. "You all right . . . Marshal?"

"I'm all right," Prophet managed, his voice pinched. He got his feet beneath him and pushed himself standing, releasing his balls, which dangled there, burning. The pain abated in increments almost too small to register. He felt the hot flash of anger unique to a man who'd been attacked in that sensitive male region.

"I can handle it now," he said, drawing the revolver from his holster and staring hotly at Miss Diamond, who cowered behind the others.

The man asked, "You want I should lock these others in the next room?"

Prophet's eyes rolled around as he tried reorienting himself against the ringing in his ears and the pain in his loins and lip. "I reckon that would be a good idea," he allowed, his voice sounding to him like a distant chirp.

"All right, ladies, you heard the marshal," ordered the man. "In the other room. Let's go, or I'll drop the hammer on you. Oh, pipe down! *Move!*"

When the man and the other three women had left, the women throwing caustic looks at Prophet and concerned ones at Lola, Prophet started toward her. She backed up against the bureau and crossed her arms defiantly across her chest. "I refuse to go anywhere with you, marshal or not."

"So you said." Prophet quickly holstered his pistol, grabbed the girl, and tossed her facedown on the bed.

"How dare you!"

"Oh, I dare, lady—I dare," Prophet snarled, grabbing a towel from the commode stand.

Towel in one hand, he wrenched one of the girl's arms behind her back and knotted the towel around her wrist. She screamed and cursed and kicked, but Prophet had her pinned to the bed with his knees. Swinging his arm out, he grabbed her other flailing hand and tied it to the first.

"You can't do this to me!" the girl shrieked so loudly that Prophet thought his eardrums would burst.

"Watch me!" With that, he grabbed another towel, looped it over her face, slid it into her mouth like a horse's bit, and tied the ends behind her head.

It didn't silence her, but it certainly piped her down.

"You see, there's more than one way to skin a cat," Prophet said, standing, jerking her off the bed, and leading her out the door. He paused to retrieve the girl's carpetbag, which she would need on the journey.

The man with the big nose was standing just outside the other room, that humorous light still flashing in his eyes. "Got her?"

"Yeah, I got her," Prophet grumbled, heading down the hall, hearing the other girls pounding on the locked door of their room.

When he was downstairs and crossing the lobby with the girl in tow, he stopped suddenly as Big Dan thundered into the building, face flushed from drink and outrage. Someone had apparently fetched him when they'd seen what was happening to his girls.

"Just *what* in the *hell* do you think you're *doin'*?" the troupe master shouted, spittle flying from his lips.

Remembering how effectively the technique had

worked for the girl, Prophet waited until Big Dan was three feet away. Then he kicked the half-drunk troupe master squarely in the balls. The man cried out, doubling over, and Prophet brought the butt of his revolver down on the back of the man's head with a resolute smack. His lights going out like a blown lantern, Big Dan hit the floor so hard that dust sifted down from the rafters.

"Now," Prophet said, regarding the other three people in the lobby, "if you'll excuse us, Miss Diamond and I have a stage to meet."

"What's this all about?" the hotel clerk inquired.

"None of your business," Prophet grouched.

Shoving the girl out ahead of him, he stepped onto the boardwalk and started across the street. He no longer cared who tried to get in his way. After what he'd been through, he was itching to shoot someone.

He didn't have to, however. Except for people stopping to stare warily at him and the gagged and bound girl, the walk to the stage office was uneventful. Fitzsimmons was conspicuously absent. Not wanting to show either involvement or uninvolvement in Prophet's kidnapping of the girl, he'd probably gone fishing.

Prophet approached the stage station just as the fresh team was being buckled into place by two wranglers. Prophet gave the tickets to the agent, who stamped them and returned them to Prophet along with the war bag, rifle, and saddlebags Prophet had left with the man earlier.

"Whatcha got goin' now, Lou?" asked the dusty driver as Prophet guided Miss Diamond to the stage. Prophet recognized Mike Clatsop, a longtime stage driver with whom Prophet had killed many a whiskey bottle and beer keg in roadhouses throughout the northern territories.

"Well, Mike," Prophet said with a weary sigh, handing over his and the girl's luggage, "Owen McCreedy wants her down in Johnson City. Don't ask me why," he added with a caustic snort.

As Prophet wrestled Lola into the coach, the driver chuckled. "With her all bound up like that, and you dressed fit to kill, I figured you musta got yourself hitched!" The guffaws rolled up from deep in Clatsop's chest.

Prophet climbed into the coach and sat beside the girl, who was still struggling with her tether and cursing him through the towel. From behind his metal cage, the station agent railed, "Pull 'em outta here, Clatsop—you're behind schedule the way it is!"

"Ah, go diddle yourself, Henry!" Clatsop retorted. He secured Prophet's and the girl's luggage in the coach's back boot, then grudgingly climbed up to the driver's box.

As he did so, Prophet drew a handkerchief from his pocket and mopped his brow and dabbed at his cracked lip. His chest was taut with strained nerves. He hadn't realized how stressful collecting bounty on one pretty redhead could be.

"Hold on!" a deep male voice called as the stage started off.

"Climb aboard, mister, but watch those wheels!" Clatsop called from the driver's box.

The door opened, and another man jumped aboard. All Prophet could see was his shoulders and bowler as he pulled himself through the door, crouching, then turned to pull the door closed behind him. The stage knocked him off balance, and he swayed this way and that, reaching for the ceiling straps. The door swung wide as the stage tilted to the right.

"I got it," Prophet said, getting up, grabbing the door, and latching it.

Grabbing the walls and ceiling straps for balance, he

struggled back into his seat. Beside him, the girl gave a sharp intake of breath, as though startled.

"What—?" Prophet started, stopping when he saw the face of the man who'd just climbed aboard.

It was the well-dressed hardcase, a grim smile stretching his thin, chapped lips and swelling the veins in his enormous nose.

6

"AIN'T THIS A coincidence?" Prophet said.

"Ain't it, though?"

"Where might you be headed?"

"Johnson City," the hardcase said, cutting his dull gray eyes at Lola, who stared at him with unadulterated hate. "I see you finally got your prisoner settled down." He grinned until his cheeks dimpled. Prophet could tell he was unaccustomed to smiling.

The bounty hunter glanced at the two Remingtons resting against the man's thighs, the man's hands not far from the gutta-percha grips. Apprehension was a bug buzzing around in the back of Prophet's head. He'd seen just too much of the man of late. Coincidence? Maybe. Henry's Crossing was a small town. While Prophet couldn't understand what business the man would have with him or the girl, he wasn't taking any chances.

"Yeah, she's a lamb," Prophet grumbled, glancing at the girl. She turned to him, eyes flaring.

"Right pretty," said the stranger.

Prophet shrugged. There was nothing like kicking a man in the balls to make a girl look ordinary. "I've seen prettier."

"Not around here you haven't."

"I'd take that towel from her mouth if she thought she could keep her mouth shut." Prophet looked at her again. She returned his gaze, containing her anger, eyes beseeching him to remove the gag.

"I don't know—wildcat, that one," the stranger said with a grin.

Prophet untied the towel from around her head. She made a dry spitting noise, as if to rid her mouth of lint, and shook her head violently, whipping her hat off. It fell on the floor. Hands tied, she left it there. She flashed her angry eyes at Prophet once more but, catching herself, said nothing.

The stranger laughed. She looked at him, then back at Prophet. The noise the stage made as it rumbled down the road was loud enough that only Prophet could hear her when she said, leaning toward him, "He's been sent to kill me."

Prophet glanced at the stranger.

"I beg your pardon?" the man said, knowing he'd been talked about.

Prophet thought for a moment, wondering how to play it. He glanced at the man's pistols again and felt a strange sensation at the base of his spine.

Deciding to play it straight—why not?—Prophet said, "The lady says you've been sent to kill her."

The man didn't say anything for about five seconds,

shifting his gaze between Prophet and the girl. "Who would send me to do that?"

"Billy Brown," the girl said.

"Who's Billy Brown?" the man asked her, beating Prophet to the punch.

"You know who Billy Brown is as well as I do," she said disdainfully, blue eyes flashing fire. "He's the bastard who cut Hoyt Farley's throat in his own saloon. He's the man who hired you to kill me before I could testify against him."

Keeping both eyes on the stranger, Prophet tensed. He found himself admiring the girl's sand. If she really thought the man had been sent to kill her, it took guts to face him down like this. But maybe she didn't think she had anything to lose. . . .

The man was staring at her, brows furrowed. He turned his head to one side, regarding her askance. "Miss, I don't have the foggiest notion what you're talking about." His eyes slid to Prophet. "Do you, Marshal?"

Prophet didn't say anything for several seconds. "Who's Hoyt Farley?" he asked Lola, keeping his eyes on the stranger, watching his hands without staring at them directly. He figured the man would telegraph any move with his eyes.

She jerked a look at him. "You don't know?"

He flushed, hesitating, feeling the girl's hot gaze on him. Apparently, a U.S. deputy marshal involved in the case would know the name of Hoyt Farley. "Hey, I'm just . . . just . . . transporting a witness to a county sheriff."

A knowing grin pulled at the nostrils of the stranger's large, pitted nose.

"He's the saloon-keeper Billy Brown killed," the girl said impatiently.

"Saloon-keeper?" the stranger said, shuttling what appeared a genuinely baffled gaze between Prophet and Miss Diamond.

"Saloon-keeper?" the girl mocked him, not buying his performance—if a performance it was. Prophet couldn't decide. He didn't know either one of these people well enough to read them.

To the girl, he said with a heavy sigh, "So . . . you're saying Billy Brown sent this man to keep you from talking to Owen McCreedy."

"That's exactly what I'm saying. Now do you see the danger you've put me in? I just hope you're better at handling your six-gun than you were at arresting me."

Prophet flushed, not at all liking how complicated his life had suddenly become. He didn't like the girl, and he didn't like the stranger sitting across from him. Situations like this were hard on a man's self-respect, not to mention his nerves.

"I don't know what she's talkin' about," the man said to Prophet. "My name's Bannon and I'm just headin' for the faro tables down in Johnson City." He stopped as a thought came to him. "Oh, I know . . . it's these Remingtons," he said, indicating the two irons on his hips. He chuckled and gave his head a wag. "Yeah, these two ladies—Ruth and Alice, I call 'em—they're mostly for show, if you know what I'm sayin'. I'm in the poker profession—a gamblin' man—and you'd be surprised all the ornery bastards I have to contend with."

"That right?" Prophet said.

"Sure. I mean, hell, when you rake the felt of someone's hard-earned cash, well, you better look out. Especially if they've been drinkin'. They're liable to pull on you—especially if they don't think you're handy with iron. I have to make it look as though I'm handy." He patted one of the gutta-percha grips lovingly. Prophet's heart thumped, and he slid his hand closer to the butt of the forty-five on his right hip.

"Easy there, pard," the man said, detecting the movement. "Don't get itchy."

"I won't if you won't."

Bannon's voice was even, his expression cool. "I was just explainin' why the girl's afraid."

"Well, why don't we just leave Ruth and Alice alone for now?"

A thin voice rose above the knock and rattle of the stage and the sharp reports of the driver's blacksnake. "I second that motion." Prophet and Bannon turned to the wizened old man sitting on the other side of Miss Diamond. He was staring at them warily, obviously in no mood to see lead flung around the coach's tight quarters.

It was the first time Prophet was more than vaguely aware of others aboard the stage. In addition to the old man, there was a middle-aged woman and a boy who appeared to be traveling together. The boy sat to Bannon's right, directly across from Miss Diamond. The woman sat next to the window, on the other side of the boy. Fear shone brightly in her eyes, but the boy shuttled his eager gaze between Prophet and Bannon, apparently not the least bit wary of a lead swap. He seemed to be thoroughly enjoying the festivities.

Prophet tipped his hat to the woman and the boy, smiling reassuringly, then looked at Bannon, who returned his gaze with a benign smile. Prophet wondered if the man was telling the truth. Was he lying, or did Miss Diamond have an overactive imagination? She *was* an actress.

For the sake of the others, Prophet extended his hand. "Lou Prophet."

Bannon shook it. "Wayne Bannon."

"Nice to meet you, Wayne."

"Likewise."

"And . . . uh . . . thanks for your help back in the hotel." Prophet offered a sheepish smile.

Bannon shrugged. "I was just passin' by and heard the commotion, that's all."

"You were stayin' at the Waddy's, eh?"

"I'm a regular there." Bannon looked at Miss Diamond and touched his hat brim. "Sorry about your trouble, ma'am. I hope everything works out in your favor."

She sneered at him, then turned away to gaze hatefully out the window.

"Game of cribbage?" Bannon asked Prophet after they'd ridden another mile or so in silence. He produced a cribbage board from an inside pocket of his frock coat.

Prophet hesitated. Then he shrugged. What better way to keep an eye on the man's hands? "Sure."

The man had handily won two rounds and was well on his way to winning a third when the stage slowed to a halt and the driver called down, "Horse rest! Fifteen minutes to stretch!"

When the stage had come to a complete stop, Prophet opened the door. He had started to get out when Miss Diamond said, "Wait. Why don't you let him go first?"

Prophet glanced at Bannon, who shrugged and chuckled. "Sure, I'll go."

Bannon climbed out. Prophet followed, then turned to help Lola, the boy, and the middle-aged woman. The old man came out last, wagging his head. "I thought for sure you two were going to have a shootin' match in there."

"This man causin' trouble, Pop?" rumbled a guttural voice behind Prophet.

Prophet turned to see Frank Harvey, a former bounty hunter Prophet had known and hated for years. They'd fought in most of the saloons between Milestown and Dodge City, and the score was about even. Prophet had heard that the man had started riding shotgun for a stage company. It would have to be this one. He just hoped Harvey didn't mention anything about bounty hunting in front of the girl. He wanted her to believe he was a deputy marshal for as long as possible.

"Hi, Frank. How you doing?"

"You causin' trouble on this here stage?" Six-six and broad as a barn, the rolled-up sleeves of his threadbare long johns revealing a maze of tattoos on his post-sized arms, Frank Harvey stood holding a double-barreled shotgun across his chest. His thick, curly beard was covered with clay-colored dust, and his floppy hat looked as though he stomped and pissed on it regularly.

"Not a bit, pard," Bannon intervened. "There was a misunderstanding a few miles back, but it was all my fault. I have a short fuse, you see, but I'm much better now." He reached into his frock coat and produced a flat silver box. "Cigarillo? They're Cuban."

Harvey's eyes were still on Prophet, like those of a half-wild dog bristling for a fight. His nose worked as he smelled the expensive tobacco, however, and his gaze gradually drifted from Prophet to the cigarillos. "Yeah . . . all right," he chafed, selecting a smoke with his sausage fingers.

"Good man," Bannon said, leading Harvey away as though attracting a dog with a bone.

Prophet gave a slow sigh of relief.

"You're right popular today, Marshal," the girl quipped. Giving her back to him, she said, "Would you mind releasing me, so I can tend to nature?"

Reluctantly, Prophet cut the tether with his Arkansas toothpick. There was no sign of the other three passengers, who'd wandered off to answer their own nature calls.

"Just remember," Prophet scolded, "there ain't nowhere to run out here. Besides, I'm a pretty fast runner myself."

He was taken aback by the brazen look she returned.

"You know, Marshal," she said with an exaggerated air of perplexity, "I never did get a very good look at that badge of yours."

"Huh?"

"Why don't you wear your badge out where folks can see it?"

Prophet looked down at his chest, his vision beginning to swim as his nerves started dancing once more. "Well . . . 'cause . . . uh . . ." For the life of him, he couldn't come up with an answer. Fidgeting, he glanced at the driver, grateful to see he was on the other side of the team, checking the horses' hooves for loose nails and shoe wear.

"Let me see your badge," Miss Diamond demanded, marching forward and yanking the right side of his coat back, revealing the badge. She leaned in close and squinted her eyes. "Huh! This doesn't look very professional at all. Why, this badge is upside down!" Her voice was an ax, chopping him in two.

"Uh . . . well . . ."

"And you know what else?" She jerked another look at the badge, pantomiming another close inspection, then returned her vilifying gaze back to Prophet. "It's not a deputy U.S. marshal's badge at all. It's a deputy sheriff's star." She waited, her eyes wide and expectant, chest heaving, her face flushed with anger.

Prophet stood there, an oversized schoolboy caught looking up girls' dresses on the playground. He didn't know what to say. His mouth opened several times before he managed to get words through it. "It . . . is . . . ?"

"Yes, it is," she said so tightly Prophet thought her jaws would crack. "Hmmm." She put a finger to her lip, mimicking deliberation. "What do you suppose that means? That—maybe, possibly—*you're not actually who you say you are*?"

Prophet could not meet her gaze. Slowly, he removed the star from his vest and tossed it in the dust. "All right," he said. "You got me. I'm not a deputy U.S. marshal."

"A deputy sheriff?" she mocked.

"I'm not a deputy sheriff, either. I'm . . ." He didn't know how to say it. He was afraid that once she learned his true profession, she'd kick him in the balls again.

"Yes?" she said, crossing her arms over her breasts, waiting.

"I'm a bounty hunter."

He looked at her. She just stood there, arms crossed, hair beneath her hat lifting slightly in the breeze, staring at him as though at a mildly interesting statue.

"But the subpoena is one hundred percent real," he assured her. "The sheriff from Johnson City hired me to issue it and to see that you made it to his office. And that's what I intend to do." His features grew stern as he touched the butt of his Peacemaker, hoping to defuse any idea she had about attacking him. He wondered how many times he could dust off his dignity before there was nothing left to dust off. In ten years of dogging badmen, he'd never felt this uncomfortable. Oh, to be rid of this woman!

She stared at him thoughtfully. "Well, you're a big man, Mr. Prophet, so there's little I can do against you. All I can do is try to convince you that if you go through with this, you and I are both going to die."

It was Prophet's turn to look skeptical. "Don't you think you might be just a little too emotional?"

"You don't believe our Mr. Bannon is out to kill me?"

"I didn't say that . . ." But he was skeptical. He'd known a lot of short-trigger men, but Bannon didn't seem the type. He was no doubt handy with his Remingtons, but he was a cardman first, a killer only in a pinch.

Miss Diamond started to respond but was interrupted by the driver approaching with a shoe hammer in his hand. Prophet saw that the other three passengers had returned but were lingering several yards away, near the back of the coach. Having overheard the argument, they were glancing guardedly at him and Miss Diamond.

"Okay, folks," the driver called. "Time to board up."

The girl looked around. "Where's Bannon?"

"He's by the tree, smoking with my pal Harvey," Prophet said.

She turned to the driver, who was returning his hammer to a tool box. "Driver, I haven't taken my comfort yet. I'll be just a minute."

The driver turned his head and frowned, but before he could say anything, she was already addressing Prophet. "You keep an eye on Bannon." Then she headed east around the rocks.

"Women," the driver said, drawing on his cigarette.

"I'll say," Prophet agreed.

They stood there smoking and chatting, Prophet keeping one eye skinned on Harvey and Bannon smoking by a tree several yards away. He wasn't concerned about Miss Diamond trying to escape him out here, for on foot she would have been in more trouble away from him than she was with him. Finally, he saw her returning, holding her dress up as she moved through the tall grass.

"What are you gawkin' at?" Prophet turned to see Frank Harvey standing behind him. The driver had gone around to mount the stage on the opposite side.

"None of your goddamn—"

"Climb aboard, Prophet, or you're gonna be sportin' this up your ass," Harvey said, holding up his double-barreled shotgun for Prophet's inspection.

"Boys, boys," Miss Diamond scolded, stepping between them.

"Let me give ya a hand there, miss," Harvey said, offering a paw.

"Thank you."

Prophet rolled his eyes as she took the shotgun rider's hand. She stumbled. "Oh, darn!" she exclaimed. "My shoe."

She bent down just as a gun popped. A bullet whistled through the air where her head had been a moment before, and plunged into Frank Harvey's chest with a thump.

7

HARVEY GRUNTED AND stiffened as he shuffled back against the stage.

"Everybody down!" Prophet yelled. As several more shots thundered, the slugs sizzling through the air to thump into the stage and ring off the iron-rimmed wheels, Prophet grabbed the girl and shoved her down behind a rock.

Crouching beside her, he drew his six-gun. Four more bullets spanged off the rock in quick succession, whining and echoing throughout the spoon-shaped valley. Rock shards rained. The older woman screamed, and Mike Clatsop bellowed curses from behind a boulder six feet from Prophet and the girl. The horses were fussing and stomping, threatening to bolt. The jehu drew his revolver and loosed a shot westward. Behind his rock, Prophet couldn't see what the driver was shooting at, but he knew it was Bannon.

"Where is he, Mike!"

"Behind that rock out yonder—thirty yards, *the son of a bitch*!" Clatsop loosed another round. Bannon responded with two rounds of his own, but they were aimed at Prophet and the girl, not Clatsop.

"He wants you bad, son!" the jehu yelled at Prophet.

Hunkered down beside him, cowering, Miss Diamond screamed, "I told you, you stupid son of a bitch!"

Ignoring her, Prophet slid a look around his rock. There were several boulders and shrubs strewn down the side of a butte before him. He detected movement behind one and was about to shoot when Bannon bounded up from behind the rock. Prophet aimed quickly and fired. The slug kicked up dust about a foot beyond the gunman, who disappeared behind more boulders and shrubs. Prophet knew he'd be heading down the crease between the two buttes behind him. He was apparently trying to escape the scene of the botched assassination, and there was nowhere else to go.

Prophet looked at the girl, curled in the fetal position with her arms over her head. "Stay down. He could circle back." Bounding out from behind the rock, he yelled, "Stay with the stage, Mike! I'm going after that bastard."

He ran past Bannon's boulder, following the flattened weeds through the shrubs and into the crease between the buttes. Bordered on both sides by more rocks, scraggly, waist-high weeds, and gnarled chokecherry shrubs, the crease led down a steep grade to an arroyo. Prophet followed the grade to the bottom of the arroyo—slowly, shrugging away tree limbs, wary of an ambush.

A spring runoff gurgled. Tracks of deer and coyote scored the soft mud. Walking with his gun held before him, Prophet came upon the prints of high-heeled boots.

Cautiously, swinging his head from left to right, Prophet followed the prints along the arroyo. Firs, box elders, and aspens grew along the sides—thick in places, thinner in others. The faint scent of pine mixed with that of the acrid water. A shrill cry rose, and Prophet ducked, jerking a look to his right. A magpie lifted off a pine branch about halfway up the rocky bank, the vacated branch bobbing behind it, the magpie careening up and behind Prophet, screeching.

Prophet swallowed, sighed, and gave his eyes back to the trail. It followed the soft sand and dirt at the bottom of the arroyo for another thirty yards, ending abruptly near a deadfall aspen. The last two boot prints stared up at Prophet tauntingly.

Where the hell . . . ?

He saw movement out of the corner of his left eye. Wheeling, he felt a bullet burn his temple at the same moment he heard the report and saw the smoke and fire stab from a gun. For a split second, the smoke and fire and the burning pain in his head enveloped him. It did not freeze him, however. As if of its own accord, his right hand brought the Peacemaker up level with Bannon's chest. It jumped as it fired.

Bannon flew back against the massive, cracked wall of granite behind him, face pinched with pain. He started bringing his gun up again, and Prophet's second shot took him through the soft skin beneath his chin, blasting through the crown of his skull, carrying jellied brains through the exit and plastering them on the granite slab above him. What remained of Bannon toppled back toward Prophet, who stepped aside as Bannon fell face first in the tracks he and Prophet had made at the bottom of the arroyo.

"There you go, you son of a bitch."

Prophet touched his temple and saw the blood on his finger. He traced the burn along his forehead. Deciding the groove wasn't deep enough to worry about, he dabbed at it with his bandanna as he went through Bannon's pockets, collecting a comb, a pencil, two packs of cards, the cigarillos and cribbage board, matches, and a roll of two hundred and fifty dollars bound with a diamond-studded money clip. Gambling winnings, no doubt. There was no indication of why he was here or who had sent him.

Billy Brown?

Prophet unbuckled the man's gunbelt, collected both Remingtons, and headed back toward the stage. He intended to give Bannon's personal effects to the first sheriff he found. Then he'd cable Owen McCreedy a very short note: "WHAT IN THE HELL IS GOING ON?"

He'd come to the place where he and Bannon had descended the arroyo when the stage driver appeared, catstepping sideways down the bank, a rifle in his hands. When he saw Prophet he stopped abruptly, one foot nearly sliding out from under him. "You find him?"

"He's dead."

Clatsop sighed and shook his head. "What the hell?"

"That's what I'd like to know," Prophet grumbled as he brushed past the jehu and continued along the trail toward the stage.

As he approached the coach, he saw the older woman, the boy, and the old man lying chest down behind a wheel, worried faces lifted toward Prophet. Seeing the bounty hunter, they looked somewhat relieved but made no effort to come out from behind the wheel. The horses were skittish, but the stage's brake had held.

Frank Harvey was sitting near the others, propped against a wheel, head inclined on a shoulder, eyes half-open, hands crossed on his lap. The snakes tattooed on both arms coiled demonically, spitting flames. Blood made a dark red bib on his chest.

"The driver said he's deader'n a doornail," the boy told Prophet eagerly.

"Daniel, you hush!" the old woman screeched.

"It's all clear," Prophet told them.

"You get him?" the old man rasped.

"Yep."

Prophet turned to the girl. She sat with her back to the rock Prophet had flung her behind. Her elbows rested on her upraised knees, and her face was in her hands.

"It's all right now—you can get up," Prophet told her.

Lowering her hands, she turned to him, eyes bright with wrath. "It's all right?"

"Yes."

Slowly, she stood—a lioness uncoiling from her resting spot to pounce on prey. There was so much fury in her bearing that Prophet felt his muscles tighten.

"It's all right?" she asked again, louder, voice taut as Glidden wire.

As she approached him stiffly, eyes wide, face blanched with indignation, Prophet worried about another kick. He kept his arms at his sides, ready to grab her foot if he had to.

"It's *all right*? We're all nearly killed, and you're saying it's *all right*?"

"Bannon's dead," Prophet said, annoyed.

"Yes, but how many more men has Billy Brown sent to kill me?"

Prophet gazed at her, frowning. He had to admit it was a good question. "Who's Billy Brown?" he asked.

Mike Clatsop shouldered up next to Prophet. "What's this about Billy Brown?"

The girl turned to the driver. "He's the one who sent Bannon to kill me. Bannon and a whole lot more, I'm afraid."

The driver's leathery, deep-lined face turned crimson,

his lips parting as if to respond, but no words formed. Watching him, Prophet said, "Would someone please tell me who the hell Billy Brown is!"

Under the stage, the old miner said, "What's this I'm hearin' again about Billy Brown?"

The driver turned to Prophet. "You ain't heard of Billy Brown, Lou?"

"No!" Prophet exclaimed.

Clatsop shook his head. "Well, hell . . . he's . . . just plain . . . *bad*."

Miss Diamond turned to Prophet. "He's a wealthy businessman in Johnson City who runs a corrupt syndicate. All the saloon-, brothel-, and theater-owners in town pay him a monthly fee or get burned to the ground . . . or worse. Worse is what happened to Hoyt Farley."

"You saw it?"

"Yes."

"And you went to the sheriff?"

"I wasn't that stupid. If I had, I'd be dead by now."

"Then how does the sheriff know you were a witness to this Farley fella's murder?"

The girl's voice was grimly sarcastic. "I have no idea. All I know is I was perfectly safe—until you showed up, thank you very much, Mr. Prophet."

Prophet was incredulous. "You don't think I led them to you, do you?"

"That's exactly what I think. I think word got out that the Johnson City sheriff hired you to bring me in. I think Billy Brown had you followed, and you led Bannon right to my doorstep."

Incensed, Prophet stepped toward the girl, stabbing a finger at his chest. "Listen, lady—nobody follows Lou Prophet without him knowing about it. *Nobody!*" Prophet's eyes were sharp, and his nostrils flared.

The girl wasn't backing down, however. Placing her

fists on her hips, she'd opened her mouth to respond when Clatsop intervened.

"Okay, okay," he said, waving his hands. "We'd best load ol' Frank aboard the coach and get a move on. We're a good hour behind schedule the way it is."

A half hour later, the stage pulled away from the stop. Frank Harvey was strapped to the top luggage rack, and Prophet was riding shotgun. The horses galloped, kicking dust in his face, and Clatsop encouraged them with his epithet-laced harangues. The bounty hunter brooded, silently cursing the girl and wondering what kind of hell he'd gotten himself into now.

Wondering which of Billy Brown's men would appear next . . . and when.

8

LOLA DIAMOND SAT beside the old miner and gazed out the stage window from under the bending brim of her straw hat. Suddenly aware of being watched, she turned to see the boy across from her staring at her with wide-eyed wonder. In spite of how tired and hopeless she felt, she smiled at the lad.

"Does someone *really* want to kill you?" the boy asked innocently.

"Daniel!" the mother snapped, grabbing the boy's thigh in a clawlike grip. "You mind your own business and stop staring at her. She's bad!"

The miner looked up from the dime novel he'd been reading. "Now, Mrs. Phelps, just because the girl's in trouble doesn't mean she's bad."

"Oh, doesn't it?" the woman said sharply. "I know who she is. She's a showgirl." The prudish, cow-eyed gaze switched to Lola, who found herself recoiling from it. "I saw her riding into Henry's Crossing with those show wagons. Harlots, all of 'em! Besides, any woman caught up in the misdeeds of badmen is bound to be bad herself. Harumph!"

"Now, Mrs. Phelps—" the miner continued placatingly.

"That's all right, mister . . . really," Lola said, offering the man an appreciative smile. "I'm used to it."

"Used to getting innocent people killed, no doubt, too," Mrs. Phelps mumbled under her breath as she gazed out her window.

Lola turned to the boy, who was staring at her again. For the boy's benefit, she stuck her tongue out at the woman, and grinned at the lad. The boy mimicked her, covering his mouth to muffle a snicker. Lola winked at him, then returned her gaze out the window, at the grassy buttes and pine-studded ridges rolling under big, puffy clouds.

She rested against the side of the coach, her mood souring quickly as she considered her situation: nabbed by a bounty hunter determined to drag her back to Johnson City. She doubted she'd get that far. If Billy Brown got his way—and when did he not?—she'd be dead very soon indeed.

How had she gotten to this horrible place in her life? she wondered. She'd been taught by the best drama teachers in the East. She was beautiful, talented, and eager to spend her life doing what she loved: singing, dancing, and acting. She belonged on the best stages in the world reciting Shakespeare, singing the best ballads to the best crowds, performing uproarious vaudeville to guffawing hordes of the impeccably dressed elite. She'd sit at the tables of aristocrats, governors, generals, presidents, and kings.

Her lovers would be tall, dashing, and Italian.

When her private train car rolled into a city, she'd be greeted by marching bands, red carpets, and tall, enclosed carriages driven by fawning men in high hats and white gloves. In the grandest hotels, the world's best champagne would await her on ice.

That was the life of an Amber Skye or a Lola Diamond. Not this traveling from one rat-bit mining dump to another in a creaking, smelly wagon led by a drunk lech like Big Dan Walthrop, only to get nabbed by some two-bit bounty hunter and hauled kicking and screaming back to a town that wanted her dead.

She couldn't have cared less about Hoyt Farley. Who was he anyway—or had he been—but some small-time brothel pimp and drink-slinger? It didn't matter to her that he was dead. She'd be damned if she'd endanger her life just to keep the man who'd killed him behind bars.

As soon as she could, she would run. Run where, she did not know. But the big, half-witted bounty hunter who'd latched onto her like a bramble burr would surely get her killed if she did not escape him soon. She was lucky to have lived as long as she had. Billy Brown's hired gun had obviously found her by following the unwitting Prophet right to her doorstep.

Damn that bounty hunter!

But how did Bannon know the sheriff of Johnson City had hired Prophet . . . unless the sheriff or someone close to him had leaked the information to Billy Brown?

She closed her eyes and shook her head to rid herself of the distressing, convoluted thoughts. All she knew for sure, and all she needed to know to stay alive, was that she was a target. The only way she'd stay alive was if she got far, far away from here . . . back to San Francisco, maybe. Or maybe she'd go down to Texas. She'd heard there were scads of show troupes down there. In one of

those, eventually, she'd roll into the fame that was right-
fully hers.

Surely Billy Brown's tentacles wouldn't reach her in
Texas. . . .

Another thought occurred to her that made her heart
quicken and her eyes darken. All she had for money was
six dollars and a few cents in her carpetbag—enough to
buy her a couple of meals, but that was all. Certainly not
enough for stage fair to San Francisco or Abilene.

As if out of nowhere, tears flooded her eyes. Feeling
her heart and soul shrivel, feeling more alone and way-
ward than she'd felt since her mother died, she lowered
her head to her hands and sobbed. It was as though she
were a dry stick broken in a hard wind, all her hopes and
dreams scattered like so much flotsam in a hurricane.

"Ah, miss, don't . . . don't do that," the old miner beseeched her.

"I'm sorry," she said, her hand over her mouth.

"It's . . . really . . . Ever'thing's gonna work out just
fine."

"Yes . . ."

"You'll see."

"I know," she said, accepting the handkerchief he offered. She wiped her eyes and blew her nose. Looking
up, she saw the boy's mother staring at her derisively.

"Yeah," the woman said. "Everything's gonna work
out just fine for her. Just fine in *hell*, that is!" With that,
she turned her head sharply back to the window.

"Oh, *Mrs. Phelps*!" the old miner chastised.

The woman acted as if she hadn't heard the man. She
continued gazing primly out the window, her gaudy coif-
fure secured beneath her cheap, feathered hat. It was the
hard set of the woman's persnickety double chin, the pug,
upturned nose, and dull eyes that saved Miss Lola Diamond from total defeat. Watching the woman in all her

disdain—a drummer's wife, probably, or a store clerk's—
filled Lola with a disdain of her own. The anger seethed
up from her toes to her legs to her stomach and chest,
until she was suddenly, inexplicably steeled by it.

A woman like Mrs. Phelps would, in a few years, be
salivating over newspaper accounts of the bewitching actress known as Lola Diamond.

With that satisfying thought, Lola gave her nose another blow, dabbed at her cheeks, and returned the handkerchief to the old miner with a grateful smile. "Yes, I
know it will, sir. Thank you." Turning to the woman
staring out the window, she lifted her chin high and said
again, cheerfully, "Thank you very much. It will indeed."

She inhaled deeply and, relaxing her shoulders, gave
the boy a wink. She returned her gaze to the countryside
rolling past the window, and considered her options. Ad-
mittedly, there were few. But when she found one—
when she found a way to escape the unsavory Lou
Prophet—she'd grab it like a rope at the bottom of a well.

"Yes," she told herself, a wistful light entering her
eyes. "Everything is going to be just fine."

That wasn't what Owen McCreedy, sheriff of Johnson
City, was thinking at the moment.

He stood looking out the window of his small sheriff's
office and jail, the draw ring of the shade hanging just
above his black felt Stetson. He watched Hart Baldridge
heading this way, a black-suited figure catching the
golden rays of the dying sun on his shoulder. Paper fluttered in the lawyer's right hand as he swerved to avoid
a puddle left by the rainstorm that had roared through
town a few hours ago. Puffing proudly on a stogy, Baldridge approached the jailhouse and bulled his way
through the door.

"Knock-knock," he said with an impudent smile.

"Why don't you try it for real sometime?" McCreedy said.

The fat end of Baldridge's cigar reddened as he drew on it, blowing smoke out the right side of his mouth. He was a tall, heavyset, hog-jowled man with black mutton-chops and wire-rimmed spectacles that hung perpetually down his nose. A barber tended him daily, and he always smelled sweetly of lavender and expensive tobacco.

"Why bother knocking? You've been watching me come for the last two blocks."

" 'Cause it's the polite thing to do," the sheriff said tensely, showing his teeth.

He'd been as wired up as an Indian wagon for the past week, his nerves shot from worry and lack of sleep. Worry over the girl . . . wondering if Prophet would get here alive . . . worry over his deputy, who'd seen Brown and two of his thugs leave Farley's saloon the night Farley was killed, chasing the girl down an alley . . . and worry over himself.

McCreedy had always fancied himself a brave man—in his prime, he'd fought Indians on the cattle trails up from Texas—but he couldn't sleep for thinking Billy Brown's hired guns were going to storm in and fill him with lead. He was also worried they'd find his wife, whom he'd secreted away at a friend's farm south of town when all the trouble had started. If they got their hands on Alice, there was no telling what those savages might do.

Reading the sheriff's mind with a mocking, self-satisfied grin on his fat face, Hart Baldridge said, "You know, you'd be doing yourself a big favor if you just forgot about this thing. Who was Hoyt Farley, anyway, but a simpleminded barman? You were no friend of his, he of yours."

"No, but he is the man whose murder I'm finally gonna

use to put away Billy Brown for good," McCreedy said, getting up close to Baldridge's face in spite of the sickly sweet stench of the man. "He's the man whose murder I'm gonna hang your client with . . . once and for god-damn all!"

"Easy, easy, Sheriff," the lawyer said, holding up his small, fat hands, palms out, and taking two steps back. "You're getting very close to assault. You wouldn't want that additional complication, now, would you?"

"To tell you the truth, I'd like nothing better," Mc-Creedy growled.

He hated the lawyer almost as much as he hated Billy Brown, and not only because Baldridge was representing the cold-blooded killer and local crime boss who had plagued McCreedy since the very day the sheriff had taken office two and a half years ago. McCreedy hated Baldridge because Baldridge thought he was as much above the law as Billy Brown did. But at the same time, the attorney never hesitated to use the statutes to his best advantage, to hide himself and Brown behind them whenever McCreedy got too close.

"Now, now," Baldridge admonished. "Temper, tem-per." He thrust the stogy into his mouth and gave several satisfied puffs, savoring McCreedy's discomfort. He looked around. "Say, your deputy get back yet . . . from his hunting trip?" His eyes cooled as a smirk toyed with his lips.

"Not yet," McCreedy snarled.

He'd sent his deputy, Perry Moon, into the mountains, to get him out of town. He was afraid that Billy Brown's men would kill the young deputy to keep him from tes-tifying against him, about what he saw the night Farley was killed: Billy Brown and his thugs running out the back of Farley's Saloon, chasing a sobbing girl down the alley.

Apparently, the girl had witnessed the killing. That's why she was indispensable to the case against Brown. The deputy's testimony would be circumstantial. Perry had seen Brown and his men leaving the saloon right after Farley was killed, but he hadn't seen the actual killing. The girl had. Only her testimony could convince a jury beyond a reasonable doubt.

Fortunately, she'd given Brown the slip. Unfortunately, she'd given McCreedy the slip, as well. He'd figured out who she was, however, when the master of a traveling theatrical troupe reported one of his girls missing—a Miss Amber Skye, the name the girl had been going by in Johnson City—the next day. McCreedy had cabled every sheriff in the territory to keep an eye out for her, not really expecting to find her.

He'd already resigned himself to watching Billy Brown walk away scot-free from another murder, when he got a cable from the sheriff at Millerville, reporting that he'd seen the girl McCreedy was looking for, and that she, now known as Lola Diamond, was en route with her troupe to Henry's Crossing. Remembering that his old cowpoke buddy turned bounty hunter, Lou Prophet, had lit out for those parts, he'd sent letters to him and to the sheriff at Henry's Crossing. Prophet may have been a carousing hillbilly at heart, but he was as good a man-tracker as you'd find in the West, and he wouldn't draw as much attention as a lawman would. McCreedy just hoped he'd prove effective at nabbing a female witness who, for very good reason, was afraid for her life.

It was only after McCreedy had located the girl that he'd arrested Brown. He thought Brown might run if he knew McCreedy had a witness to the murder. He'd also thought that by locking Brown up, he might be able to keep Brown from sending someone to kill the girl. But he'd realized the folly in such a strategy the first time

Brown's lawyer visited Billy in jail. Obviously, Hart Baldridge was relaying messages to Brown's men—messages no doubt including the one to make sure Lola Diamond did not reach Johnson City alive.

McCreedy knew now that by arresting Billy Brown before he had the girl under wraps, he'd telegraphed his knowledge of the girl's whereabouts and had inadvertently endangered not only his case, but the girl's life. He'd realized this only after he'd sent Prophet the letter. For days now he'd been haranguing himself for his error, and hoping against hope that Prophet and the girl made it here alive. If they didn't, it would be McCreedy's fault.

"The hunting must be good in the mountains, eh, Sheriff?" Baldridge asked jovially, referring to McCreedy's deputy's prolonged vacation.

"Must be."

"Any luck finding the girl?"

"None whatsoever, Baldy," McCreedy lied. He knew that Baldridge and Brown knew he'd located the girl. He could see it in the smug expression on the attorney's face. What McCreedy hoped, however, was that they had not yet learned where he'd found her. Certainly they didn't know that Prophet was the man—of all people—McCreedy had sent to retrieve her. The only people who knew about that were McCreedy, the sheriff in Millerville, Sheriff Fitzsimmons of Henry's Crossing, the girl, and Prophet himself.

"Uh . . . that's Bald*ridge*."

"Sorry."

"Yes, I am, too . . . about the girl, I mean."

McCreedy shrugged, not liking the self-satisfied gaze in the attorney's eyes. Could he and Brown have located her, as well? McCreedy chastised himself once more for not warning Prophet about possible trouble. "Well, I'm still hopin' she'll turn up somewhere," he said, hiding his torment and feigning resign as he looked askance at the attorney's beady black eyes.

"Yes, well, maybe so," Baldridge said, clearing his throat. "Now then, Sheriff, I'm here to see my client."

"It's gettin' late—I'm about to close," McCreedy growled, turning to the stove for a cup of coffee.

"I'm sorry, Sheriff, but it's urgent."

"Diddle yourself."

Baldridge sighed. "Sheriff, must we go through this again? You know all I have to do is go to Judge Frye. It'll take some time, sure, but time you could otherwise be spending eating a big steak and a plate of beans . . . uh . . . if you still have an appetite, that is. . . ."

McCreedy poured coffee into a stone mug and smiled in spite of himself. "You know, Hart—you don't mind if I call you Hart, do you?—I'm really gonna love seeing you hang next to Billy. You and Billy together . . . one last time."

Baldridge sighed again and rolled his eyes. He removed the cigar from his mouth and tapped ashes on the floor. "What's it going to be, McCreedy? Do I get to see my client now or thirty minutes from now—with an order from Judge Frye?"

"Oh, go ahead . . . knock yourself out," McCreedy said resignedly, sipping from the cup. "You know where the keys are."

"Oh, for the love of—!" Baldridge marched over to McCreedy's desk, found the key ring, and opened the door to the cell block.

As he jerked the door open, McCreedy said, "Hold it, Baldy. You know the drill." He put down his coffee cup and patted down the attorney, who stood with his arms held theatrically out from his sides, head inclined, eyes rolled to the ceiling.

"All right—you're clean," McCreedy said. "But remember to put those keys back where you found them!"

Puffing with exasperation, Baldridge bolted through the door and slammed it behind him. Hearing his footsteps echoing down the cell block, McCreedy turned toward the door. The disdainful grin faded from his lips without a trace, his eyes betraying his anxiety.

He'd waited to get Billy Brown behind bars for a long time. But now that he had, he knew it could very well be the end of not only him, Owen McCreedy, but his buddy Lou Prophet and the girl, as well.

9

BALDRIDGE STOPPED AT the first cell on the left. A shaft of dying light angled through the single barred window and shone on the stout body of Billy Brown, who lay on his cot, hands behind his head, feet propped on the outside wall, ankles crossed.

Brown was smoking a hand-rolled cigarette with a bored, thoughtful air. He was a peppery little Easterner with coarse, curly gray hair and a bulldog's face and body—short, skinny legs, broad shoulders, and a hard, round paunch. The sleeves of his white silk shirt were rolled up his meaty arms, revealing the scars and tattoos harking back to the days he'd been a street fighter in Philadelphia.

Billy Brown had come up the hard way: with his fists. Now he owned three saloons and brothels here in Johnson City and two more in Skowfield, twenty miles east. Those were his legal interests. The illegal included rustling, horse stealing, whiskey- and gun-running, crooked gambling, and a healthy cut of every saloon and brothel in Johnson City, which he enforced under threat of arson and murder. His army of cutthroats numbered around twenty-five, at least twelve of whom were never allowed to show their faces in either Johnson City or Skowfield. That's how wanted they were by the law.

"That you, Hart?" he asked now as Baldridge stopped outside his door and fumbled with the keys.

"It's me, Billy. Had a little trouble with McCreedy."

"What kinda trouble?"

"Wouldn't let me in at first." Baldridge poked the key in the lock and turned it back and forth, jerking the door. "He was just throwing his weight around. He knows we've got him by the short hairs, and he's squirming to beat the band."

Brown swung his feet to the floor as Baldridge opened the door. "That goddamn McCreedy!" Brown rasped. His voice sounded like sandpaper on hardwood, and he spoke in a staccato, East Coast rhythm, his freckled, blue-eyed face pinched and red with exasperation. "The son of a bitch'll die tomorrow if I give the order."

"He knows that as well as we do, Billy," Baldridge said, tossing the keys on the cell's single small table. "But like I said before, killing the sheriff would bring the wrong kind of attention. The U.S. Marshals and the governor's office might get involved. No . . . as your attorney, I advise you to let nature run its course."

"Yeah, yeah, nature," Brown rasped impatiently, staring at the paper in Baldridge's hand. "What do you have?"

Baldridge pulled the ladder-back chair away from the table, upon which a game of solitaire had been abandoned, as well as a cup of cold coffee and an ashtray filled with cigarette butts. The lawyer sat down, the chair creaking beneath his considerable girth. A cool smile played over his heavy, shiny face as he handed the papers to his boss.

"Bannon found the girl."

Brown grabbed the cable. "You shittin' me?"

"He was the man to send. Said he has a snitch in Henry's Crossing. We'll need to send money to pay this snitch for his services."

Billy Brown grinned at the attorney. He leaned toward the man and pinched Baldridge's cheeks until the attorney's eyes watered. "You were right about Bannon—you lard-ass son of a bitch!" He released the attorney and rubbed his hands together eagerly, squealing like a pig. His cheeks were crimson. "He kill her yet?"

"No," Baldridge said, kneading his sore cheeks. "He cabled from Henry's Crossing. He's hopping the stage with her and some bounty hunter who picked her up to bring her back here." Baldridge smiled with his eyes. "Apparently, McCreedy found her, too."

"Well, when's he gonna kill her?"

"Somewhere between Henry's Crossing and the first stage stop."

"How's he gonna do it?"

"Didn't say."

Billy Brown stood and walked to the window. One tattooed arm on the ledge, he sucked nervously on the quirley, thinking. His eyes darted around in their tiny sockets, like blue rats in a cage. "We have any other men in the area?"

"Six. Morgan and Price are at the gold camp in Hutton. Dick Dunbar and three others are in Elmora."

"Send 'em all over to the first overnight stop on that stage route. What is it—that the Backwater Station?"

"I believe so," Baldridge said, watching his boss curiously.

"Send them over there." Brown took a quick, deep drag on the cigarette and turned to his underling, blowing smoke through his nose and mouth. "I want them to make sure she's dead."

"I'm sure Bannon knows—"

"Yeah, yeah, I'm sure Bannon knows his job. But Bannon's only worked for me a few months. He's the Missouri gambler, ain't he? Don't know him that well. You know how I am. I just wanna be sure. Okay, Hart? Is that all right with you?"

The attorney shook his head and held up his hands placatingly. "Sure. That's fine, Billy. Whatever you say."

"And tell Morgan and Price to kill Bannon." The agitated Brown made a slashing motion across his throat. He was breathing heavily now, sweat beading his broad, freckled forehead.

Baldridge feared him when he got this excited. No telling what the squirrely son of a bitch might do. Baldridge nodded, making every effort to appease the man.

"Absolutely, Billy. You got it. I'll cable them tonight."

It was a reasonable precaution, he had to admit. Why take a chance on the man getting caught and squawking? Baldridge didn't think it possible with Bannon, from what he'd heard about the gambling gunman, but if Billy wanted him dead, the man would die.

"That's more like it. Now tell me who she's with."

Baldridge frowned. Billy had gotten him too nervous to follow the broken strands of the conversation. "Who's with who?"

"The girl!"

"Oh . . . uh, some bounty hunter." Baldridge glanced at the paper crumpled in Billy's meaty fist. The Irishman had been too agitated to read Bannon's telegram. "Prophet, I think, is his name."

"Prophet, huh?" Billy grouched, turning back to the

window and taking a sharp drag on the quirley, which was about the size of a thumbnail. He preferred cheap, hand-rolled cigarettes to the expensive cigars he could afford. Probably a habit he couldn't kick from the old, street-fighting days in the city. One of many, Baldridge speculated, his mind flashing on the men Brown had beaten to death with his fists, their faces pummeled to burger.

"At least Prophet *was* his name—right, Billy?" Baldridge said, pulling a funny.

When Brown only grunted, staring out at the side street where horsemen and wagons passed and store owners closed their doors and started home for supper, Baldridge stood. "Well, I'll go and fire a cable off to Morgan and Price, tell 'em you want Bannon dead—if you're sure that's what you want. He's a good man."

"I want him dead!" Brown barked.

"Then he's dead, Billy."

"And Prophet and the girl!"

"And Prophet and the girl—of course, Billy."

Baldridge turned to the door. He swung it open and stepped through. Locking it, he regarded his boss guiltily, cursing McCreedy for making him lock the door himself. The sheriff knew that Billy Brown, simple barbarian that he was, would hold it against him, never mind that Baldridge had no other choice in the matter.

And that's just how Billy stared at him now, too, his bulldog's nose wrinkling, brows lowering, cigarette stub smoldering in the corner of his mouth.

Baldridge tried a smile, tipped his hat, and hurried back toward the office. The hair on the nape of his neck stood straight up in the air.

10

THE SUN HAD been down for an hour, the sky awash with stars, when the stage wheeled around a butte and several pole corrals. It pulled to a halt before the station, an inky black, two-story smudge around four lantern-lit windows.

A dog had run out from the shadows to nip at the wheels and bark. Now it ran excitedly under the idle coach, panting, tail-wagging, waiting for the door to open and the passengers to climb out.

"Well, that was an entertaining ride," Prophet told the jehu wryly, casting a cautious glance at the building looming on his right. If one gunman had been sent, so could two, three, and who knew how many more?

"Yeah . . . thanks to you and that girl," Clatsop said sourly, wrapping the reins around the brake.

"Sorry, Mike."

"Not that I ever took a shine to ole Frank, but shotgun

riders ain't easy to find in this hell-for-leather country."
He called down to the passengers, "Night stop!"

Gripping the shotgun in both hands, Prophet climbed
down from the driver's box and opened the coach door.
He offered his hand to Miss Diamond, but she ignored
him and headed for the luggage boot. He was still helping
Mrs. Phelps when the showgirl mounted the porch steps
with her carpetbag.

"Wait," he told her. "Why don't you let me check it
out first?"

While Clatsop helped the others find their bags in the
luggage boot, Prophet mounted the steps, on which Miss
Diamond had stepped to one side and froze. Prophet
opened the door and went in. He was met in the long
front room crowded with oilcloth-covered tables by a
heavy-set woman in an apron. The air smelled like beef
and biscuits.

"The stage is late this evenin'," the woman said, wip-
ing her hands on the apron. Her hair was falling out of
its bun. "The roast is cooked dry."

An old, scarecrow man in coveralls and two stringbean
boys sat at one of the tables, pie and coffee before them.
They watched Prophet expectantly. He turned to the
woman. "Any strangers here?"

The woman wrinkled her brows curiously, then
laughed. "Just you!"

"You have a room for a young lady?"

"There's five rooms upstairs. She can take her pick."

"Obliged," Prophet said.

As he turned back to the door, the old man said, "You
ridin' shotgun? Where's Frank?"

"Dead," Prophet said, too tired to explain.

The door opened, and Clatsop sauntered in. Behind
him were Mrs. Phelps, the boy, and the old miner.

"Upstairs with your bags, folks," the woman scolded.

"Then come back down for food. It's pret' near cooked to leather, though. I don't know what in the world Mike Clatsop was doin' out there!"

Prophet stepped outside. "It looks safe," he told the girl, still standing on the steps. "Rooms are upstairs."

Wordlessly, she brushed by him, stepped inside, and crossed the room toward the stairs. Prophet followed her in and saw the woman, the old man, and the boys do double-takes, staring at the pretty, red-haired young woman who kept her head down as she made for the stairs, up which she disappeared, lifting the hem of her dress above her ankles. The boys, both unkept towheads, one with a fuzzy mustache, the other with a mustache and sparse muttonchops, glanced at each other with faint, lewd lights in their otherwise dull eyes.

Prophet sat at a table across from Mike Clatsop. The woman brought him a plate of food—roast beef as tough as shoe leather, boiled potatoes, canned corn, and a cold biscuit. He washed it all down with several cups of hot, black coffee, then dug into a piece of rhubarb pie the woman had brought when she'd seen him swabbing his plate with the biscuit.

The pie made up for the lackluster main course—good and sweet, with a greasy, sugary crust. Not tart, the way some rhubarb pies could be, depending on the cook. Rhubarb wasn't grown down south, and it was one of the few good things he'd found in the North. He'd vowed for years that if he married a Yankee, she'd have to bake one hell of a good rhubarb pie.

When the woman returned to take his dessert plate, she said, "Is that girl of yours gonna come down here and eat? I don't serve in the rooms—no matter how uppity they are."

"She's not my girl," Prophet said, finishing his coffee.

"She had a bad time on the trail. Why don't you fill a plate, and I'll bring it up to her?"

"She the reason Frank was killed?" the woman asked him, tilting her head to one side, a fist on her hip.

"Yeah, but it's not what you're thinkin'," Prophet said.

"I bet it's not," the woman said, then wheeled and headed back to the kitchen.

When she returned with a plate and a cup of coffee, Prophet took it upstairs, leaving his shotgun propped against the table. In the hall, lit by a single wall lamp, were five doors, two on each side, one at the end. Bedsprings squeaked briefly behind the second door on the right.

He knocked.

"Go away."

"It's Prophet."

"Go to hell!"

"I've got a plate for you."

"I'm not hungry."

"Roast beef," Prophet said enticingly.

There was no reply.

"Coffee?" he said.

After a few seconds, the bedsprings complained behind the door. Floorboards squawked. The door opened. The girl appeared. She grabbed the coffee from Prophet's hand, spilling a little, and started closing the door. Midway, she stopped. She looked down and saw her hideout gun in Prophet's hand, butt forward.

"Take it," he said. "If you use it on me, you'll be cuttin' off your nose to spite your face."

She looked at him, grabbed the gun, and slammed the door.

"Listen," he said, bowing his head at the closed door, trying to think of something to say. "I'm . . . I'm sorry about all this. I didn't know what kind of trouble you were in. McCreedy didn't tell me."

The bed sang again. The door opened a foot.

"Well, now you know, don't you?"

"You have any idea if any others are going to come?"

She smirked, her eyes almost crossing. "Oh, they'll come."

"How many?"

"However many it takes."

Prophet nodded thoughtfully.

"Going to let me go?" she asked him, lovely eyebrows arched hopefully.

"No, I—"

The door closed in his face. Doubting it would open again this evening, he went back downstairs and gave the plate to the woman, saying, "She wasn't hungry, after all." Then he grabbed his shotgun, went outside, and stood on the gallery.

He dug in his coat pocket for his makings pouch. The coach sat before him, but the horses were gone, the old man and the two boys having led them off to the barn, which hulked across the road. Light peered between the doors.

A sickle moon hung just above the peaked roof. It was butter yellow, and two bright stars hovered nearby, one of them winking like a guttering candle. The night was so still that Prophet could hear the stomping and blowing of the horses in the barn, the tin clatter of feed buckets, and the old man's gruff commands. The dog sniffed in the weeds left of the barn, making rustling noises and soft snorts as it hunted for mice.

Prophet turned sharply to his left as a loud snore rose, pumping his heart and nearly buckling his knees. It was Mike Clatsop, fallen asleep in the rocking chair, head back, jaw rising and falling as he breathed. A light in the curtained window shone on the pink pate of his bald head.

"Sorry for the trouble, old-timer," Prophet mumbled, lighting the cigarette and turning to the barnyard. He squatted on his haunches, smoking and thinking.

As many men would be sent as needed. If that was so, who would the next be and when would they come? Tonight? Tomorrow? The next day?

If that was so, why was he doing this? Why didn't he just turn the girl loose? Prophet could mail the money back. It wasn't much in the first place, and McCreedy should have told him the danger he'd face if he took the job—if McCreedy knew. But there was the problem of Prophet's debt to the Johnson City sheriff, who had saved him from a good, old-fashioned neck stretching down in Kansas, all those years ago.

Prophet brought the quirley to his lips and drew deep. Blowing smoke, he lowered his head and shook it, feeling the knot of anger and defiance in the pit of his stomach. He wasn't quitting. Not only because he'd never quit anything he'd started in his life, but because someone wanted him to.

It was his own stubborn pride that might very well get him and the girl killed, but he wasn't a quitter, and he could no more change his nature than the color of his eyes.

He finished the cigarette, stubbed it out on the ground, and retrieved his saddlebags, shotgun, and rifle from the luggage boot. He hauled them upstairs, found an unoccupied room, and changed back into his trail clothes, embarrassed about the failed ruse. What suit could hide what he was—a six-foot-three-inch, bull-necked, ham-handed Georgia hick turned witless bounty hunter? She'd seen through him from the get-go. And the badge fiasco!

"You're about as dumb as they come, Prophet," he

scolded himself, stomping into his old boots. His face cracked a smile at the snug, familiar fit of the old leather, the calluses rubbed by the others thanking him almost audibly.

Decked out in blue jeans, buckskin tunic, blue bandanna, and weather-beaten hat, he headed downstairs with the new suit and boots rolled under an arm.

"Here you go, Pop," he said to the old man washing up at the stove. "A new suit for Sundays." He tossed the clothes on a chair and walked outside.

The two boys stood beside the stage, looking up at the rooftop luggage rack, where Frank Harvey still lay, wrapped in rope. Mike Clatsop snored in the rocker.

The boys turned to him. The one with the scraggly muttonchops said, "Gramps said we're s'posed to bury him." His voice was dull, his eyes wide with apprehension.

"So you haven't seen a dead man before—that it?"

"That's right," the other boy did not hesitate to admit.

Prophet smiled. "I'll take care of it. Just hunt me up a shovel, will you?"

Prophet climbed onto the stage.

"You're gonna need help gettin' him down from there," Muttonchops said.

Prophet shook his head as he straddled Harvey's body, slipping his knife from his belt sheath. "Gettin' him up here was a bitch," he said, cutting the ropes holding Harvey to the luggage rack. "Gettin' him down's the easy part."

He resheathed his knife, grabbed an arm and a leg, and, with a grunt, rolled Harvey over the side. The dead man landed in the dirt with a heavy thud.

"Jesus, mister!" protested the boy with only the mustache.

"He's dead, for chrissakes," Prophet said. "What were

you two gonna do—bust your guts for a bag of bones?" Climbing down, he shook his head. "Never send boys to do a man's work."

Prophet stood between Frank Harvey's legs and, imitating a draft horse between two shafts, lifted the dead man's ankles to his sides. He dragged him out behind the barn, one of the boys following. When he found some soft earth over a dry creekbed, the weeds and bushes glittering in the starlight, the other boy brought a shovel, and Prophet began to dig while the two boys stood there silently watching, awfully fascinated.

When he'd dug for a short time, he handed the shovel to the boy with the muttonchops, who dug for another ten minutes.

"That's deep enough," Prophet said. He'd been smoking and keeping an eye on the yard.

He rolled the body into the grave and, cigarette dangling from his mouth, covered the hole with dirt, patted it smooth. "Well, that about does it. Wasn't so bad, eh?"

"Aren't you gonna cover him with rocks?" the boy with only the mustache asked, troubled.

"What for?"

"So critters don't dig up his bones. There's wolves prowl around here."

"They can help themselves," Prophet grunted.

He returned the shovel to the boy with the muttonchops and started back to the yard, the boys following silently behind him. When he came around the barn, he stopped suddenly, adrenaline jetting in his veins.

Two saddled horses were tied to the hitchrack before the house, lathered like they'd been ridden hard to get here.

11

SCOLDING HIMSELF FOR not keeping a closer watch on the yard—he was going to get that girl killed yet—Prophet made a beeline for the house and jerked the screen door open. Stepping inside, he raked his eyes across the lantern-lit room.

Two men, broadened by the shadows cast by the lanterns, sat at a table close to the kitchen. They were drinking coffee, and they looked up quickly as Prophet stepped into the room.

Silence yawned as the two factions regarded each other like unfamiliar dogs. The faces of both strangers were silhouetted against the lantern hanging on the wall behind them. Their hats lay on the table, their longish hair sweat-matted to their scalps. Both wore hide vests, dusters, and bandannas. Prophet couldn't see their guns, but he knew they were packing iron.

Finally, one of the newcomers said, "Hidy," and brought his cup to his lips and drank.

"Hidy," Prophet said. "Didn't know we had company."

"Just rode in," the taller of the two men said. He sat facing Prophet directly. The other man sat to his left, facing the outside wall and holding his cup to his face with both hands.

Prophet sauntered over to a table, pulled a chair out, and sat down. "Musta rode in mighty fast," he said, grinning. "Those horses are lathered a bit."

The two strangers said nothing to this. Prophet could hear someone moving around in the kitchen, opening and closing a squeaky range door.

"I'm Prophet," the bounty man said, conversationally, trying to feel the two men out, hoping they hadn't been sent for the girl, while the alarms in his head told him otherwise.

"That right?" said the tall man. He glanced at the other man; his dark eyes having acquired a humorous cast, they slid back to Prophet. "We're Smith and Jones."

He looked at his partner again and grinned. His partner laughed. He covered his mouth when the woman came out of the kitchen with an angry sigh, carrying two steaming plates. She set the plates before the men, glanced at Prophet with a scowl, then turned back toward the kitchen.

"Oh, miss," the tall man called, extending his cup. "Could I have more coffee?"

"Yeah, me, too," his partner chimed in.

The woman went into the kitchen and returned with the black enamel pot, holding the handle with a leather mitt. She slopped coffee into the men's cups while they ate.

"What about you?" she said, shooting a look across

the room at Prophet. "You want coffee, too?"

Prophet figured she couldn't get much angrier, so he went ahead and voiced his wish. "You have any o' that pie left?"

Unexpectedly, her eyes softened. "You liked that pie, did ye?"

"If you weren't already married, you would be . . . first thing in the mornin'." Prophet's eyes slitted flirtatiously.

She snickered and went into the kitchen, from which a tinny clatter issued. She reappeared a moment later with a big piece of pie and a stone mug of coffee, so black it would have floated a horseshoe.

"Much obliged, Mrs.—"

"Hill," she finished for him, her haughty demeanor returned. She set the coffee pot on the newcomers' table and addressed them automatically. "Now I'm cleaning up the kitchen and going to bed. I don't serve all night long. Help yourselves to more coffee, but when it's gone, it's gone. No gambling and no roughhousing on the premises."

With that, she tossed a lock of stray hair back from her face, returned to the kitchen, and started priming a squeaky well pump. Prophet picked up his fork and sliced into his pie, eyeing the newcomers eating with noisy abandon.

He chewed a forkful of pie thoughtfully and swallowed. "Who's Smith and who's Jones?"

The tall man looked up from his plate, both cheeks bulging as he chewed. When he opened his mouth, Prophet could see a biscuit. "He's Smith an' I'm Jones."

Prophet nodded. He forked pie into his mouth and said, "Where you from . . . Mr. Smith and Mr. Jones?"

The short man turned his head sharply to Prophet, squinting his eyes. "Well, ain't you the snoopy one!"

"Easy, Morg—" The tall man glanced at Prophet. "I

mean Jones. He's just bein' friendly, that's all. Ain't that right, Mr. Prophet?"

"That's right," Prophet said, one hand on his right thigh, close to his gun. These two looked handy with iron, but they didn't look any handier than he was. The problem was there were two of them.

"That's right," Prophet said, staring over his coffee cup. "Just bein' friendly."

Smith shoved another forkful of beef in his mouth. "Me and Jones here," he said, pausing to swallow, "we're up from Kansas . . . headin' for the gold fields west of here. Gold-seekers, you might say." He lifted his gaze to Prophet while he ate, and winked. "Hell, ever'body else is diggin' for El Dorado. Why can't we?"

"Mighty tempting, I have to admit," Prophet said. "Kansas, you say, eh?"

Smith nodded as he chewed. "Abilene. We worked for a spread thataway."

"Oh, really?" Prophet said, setting his coffee down and taking up his fork. "I worked a few spreads down there myself. The T-Bar and Hoffman's Lazy-H."

Jones glanced at Prophet, sneering, then turned to Smith. "Now I s'pose he wants to know who we rode for—snoopy bastard."

"Easy, Jones, easy," Smith said, patting his partner's wrist. To Prophet, he said, "It's getting past his bedtime. Jones always gets cranky when he's up too late."

"I see."

"We rode for a man called Breckenridge."

"Breckenridge?"

Smith was swabbing his plate. "Hear of it?"

"Sure, I heard of it," Prophet said. "That's about the biggest spread in Dawson County. At least, it used to be."

"Still is . . . as of two weeks ago," Smith said.

Prophet nodded and studied the two men warily, perplexed. They did indeed look like drovers. They might have gotten tired of the long hours, back-breaking work, and poor pay, and decided to head for the mining camps. They might have given Prophet the obviously phony names just for the fun of it. Cowboy humor. But why the lathered horses?

The bounty man knew little enough about these men to know he'd have to keep a close eye on them tonight— if they stayed over, that was, and Prophet had a feeling they would.

His suspicion was validated when Smith finished his coffee, sat back in his chair, and stretched. "Well, Jones, what you say we bed the horses down in the barn and mosey upstairs for some shut-eye?"

"I hear that."

The two men scraped their chairs back, stood, and headed for the door, Smith tipping his hat at Prophet as he passed. Prophet cracked an affable smile and offered a nod. When they were gone, he sat trying to figure a plan to protect the girl, alone in her room, with these two men in the same house.

But they didn't know what room she was in, Prophet reminded himself. Which meant they'd probably wait till morning to show their hand, when she appeared. That's when Prophet had to be ready. He wished she'd let him sleep in her room tonight, but he knew his chances of that were nil. Attempting to do so might not only get him another boot to the groin, but give her room away, as well.

He finished his coffee, went to the door, and looked out. The barn doors were open, spilling light on the hard-packed, hay-flecked earth. Deciding to head upstairs before Smith and Jones returned, to get himself situated and ready for anything, Prophet made for his room and lit the lamp on the dresser. He picked the sawed-off Rich-ards off the bed and hefted it thoughtfully in his hands.

Moving to a window, he pulled the shade away and peered down into the yard. The light in the barn went out. A moment later, Smith and Jones appeared, two dark figures heading across the yard to the house. When they were inside, boots clomping on the wood floor below, Prophet went to the door, holding the shotgun in both hands out before him, and pressed his back to the wall.

Listening through the door, he heard the men climb the stairs.

"Well, what the hell room's empty . . . ?" Smith carped.

"This one here . . . the door's open," Jones said.

It was the last room on the right, on the other side of Prophet. When Prophet heard their door close, he gave a relieved sigh and sat on the edge of the bed, listening until the noises in the next room had died. Then he pushed himself back onto the bed, his back against the headboard, boots crossed, feeling the tension ease a little.

Prophet knew he couldn't let his guard down com-pletely. It was when you thought you were in the clear that all hell broke loose.

Hours passed, slow as a lifetime. The lamp flickered and spat, then steadied for a while, flickering and spitting again intermittently, all night long. Prophet dozed lightly for a few minutes at a time, waking with a jerk, his whole body tensing, whenever someone in one of the bedrooms coughed, the old miner ceased snoring suddenly before resuming, the joists creaked as the house settled, or a mouse scuttled in the hall.

Prophet was grateful when the first light of dawn smudged his window, and the birds began stirring, their chirps and songs sounding as loud as thunder after the long, silent night. Someone in the living quarters below must have heard them, too, for they began moving around down there. When the first smell of coffee wafted up the stairs, Prophet heard the old jehu, Mike Clatsop, open his door, give a tired groan, and clomp down the hall in his boots.

"Stage leaves in forty minutes, folks!" he reported in a voice about two decibels below a yell. Then he continued downstairs.

Prophet didn't move until he'd heard Smith and Jones leave their room and stroll downstairs, spurs jangling like change. Then he got up and blew out his lamp.

His saddlebags over his left shoulder, his shotgun hanging down his back, and his Winchester in his right hand, he headed downstairs in time to see Smith head outside and Jones sit down at one of the tables. Mike Clatsop must have gone out to help the old man and the boys hitch the horses to the stage, for he was nowhere in sight. The smell of bacon and coffee was thick and enticing. Through the open kitchen door rose the sounds of cooking.

"Mornin'," Prophet said to Smith, who sat with his arms on the table before him, unshaven face puffy from his good night's rest. "Sleep well?"

Jones made a face as though he smelled shit on his boots. "Like a log," he drawled. "How 'bout you?"

"Like a dead man."

Smith came the closest Prophet had seen him to cracking a smile. Seeing the rifle and the shotgun, Smith said, "Why, you're loaded for bear!"

"Never know what, or who, you might run into out here."

Smith smirked. "Ain't that a fact?"

Mrs. Hill appeared with a coffee pot and a tray of cups. She set it all down on a table in the room's center. "Help yourselves to coffee, boys. Breakfast'll be out in a minute."

Prophet got up, poured coffee into a cup, and delivered the cup to Smith's table with a grin. "There ye are, friend," he said. "First cup's on me."

Smith looked up at him dull-eyed, contemptuous, and didn't say anything. Prophet poured himself a cup of coffee and sat down. He'd taken two sips when Mrs. Phelps and her son Daniel appeared, and took a table as far from Prophet as they could get. The old miner was about three minutes behind them, joining them at their table.

Prophet was wondering about Miss Diamond—had she overslept or snuck out a window?—when Mrs. Phelps brought a plate for him and Jones. First come, first served. The bounty man was about to get up to pour himself another cup of coffee when he saw Smith standing in the doorway. He'd froze and was looking toward the stairs.

Prophet turned to see what Smith was looking at, and his pulse quickened. Miss Diamond stood at the foot of the stairs, frozen, staring at Smith, as if some inner alarm warned her of danger.

Prophet's gaze shifted to Jones. He, too, was staring at the girl, dark eyes wide with mute excitement. Prophet's heart pounded. A warm flush spread up his neck and into his face. The Winchester stood against the wall behind him. His shotgun was strapped around his neck, hanging butt-up down his back.

He became acutely aware of the eight-gauge. Could he get to it in time, or should he go for the Peacemaker?

He shifted his gaze back to Smith, whose eyes darted between Prophet and Jones as he nervously licked his lips and slowly moved his right hand toward the revolver hanging on his thigh.

"What are we doin' here, Price?" Jones asked tightly,

gritting his teeth. Jones was watching Prophet and the girl, who remained before the stairs, frozen in place, eyes wide with trepidation.

Smith swallowed a dry knot in his throat. "I'll take Prophet," he said calmly. Then he yelled, "You take the girl!"

Jones's right arm jerked to his six-shooter. Pulling the shotgun over his head with his right hand, Prophet bounded to his feet. He got the eight-gauge out before him, thrust his right finger through the trigger guard, eared back the right hammer, leveled the barrels on Jones, and squeezed the trigger.

The shotgun roared smoke and fire, and Jones gave a high-pitched yell as the buckshot caught him in the chest, stood him up, and flung him back against the wall.

Prophet didn't see him fall. He was too busy kicking the table out to his left and diving to his right just as Smith clawed iron and loosed two quick rounds in his direction. The slugs tore into the wall behind his table. Prophet hit the floor on his right side, brought the shotgun up, earing back the left trigger, and thundered another round of buckshot toward Smith, who yelled, dropped his gun, grabbed his right shoulder, and sagged against the doorjamb.

"Goddamn, you . . . *son of a bitch!*" he cried, his face twisted in pain, blood leaking between the fingers of his gloved left hand.

He heaved himself off the jamb and ran outside. Prophet climbed to his feet, shoved a table out of his way, and ran to the door. By the time he got there, Smith had mounted one of the two horses he'd apparently saddled and led out from the barn. Sagging in the saddle of a skewbald gelding, he dug his spurs into the horse's ribs and headed out of the yard at a ground-eating gallop.

Knowing that if the man got away he'd summon others, Prophet dropped the empty shotgun, unholstered his Peacemaker, and ran out to the middle of the yard. Dropping to a knee, he fired off an entire cylinder. The last bullet took the man just under his hat. He sagged down the side of the running horse and rolled.

Prophet stood and stared at the dead man through the dust churned up by his horse, which had fled out of sight. He tipped his hat back and ran a hand down his face. He'd gotten these two, but how many more would come?

However many it takes, the girl had said.

With a sick feeling in the pit of his stomach, Prophet knew it was true.

12

PROPHET AND CLATSOP, who'd run up from the corral when he'd heard the shooting, dragged the bodies behind the barn. The boys, wizened veterans, offered to bury them beside Frank Harvey.

Since they all, including Prophet, had lost their appetites, they forwent breakfast and filed out to the stage. As the old man and the two boys backed the team between the shafts, Prophet pulled the girl aside.

"I think we'd best light out on our own," he said. "Everyone in the county knows what stage we took."

"I'll say they do," she sniped.

Prophet glanced at the Appaloosa Smith had tethered to the hitchrack before the house. "You take that horse. I'll see about rounding up one for myself."

It wasn't hard convincing the old man to lend him one of his saddle horses, tack, and a soogan. The old station agent was shaken by the shooting, and it didn't take a genius to see that the sooner Prophet and the girl were gone, the better off everyone would be.

Mike Clatsop didn't argue with the decision, either.

"Prophet, I hope you make it," the jehu said from atop the driver's box, looping the reins in his arthritic old hands. "But I gotta tell you, if you're in trouble with ole Billy Brown, you prob'ly won't."

"Thanks for the note of encouragement," Prophet said as he walked a saddled speckle-gray up from the barn.

"If I was you, I'd head north to Canada," Clatsop continued. "The winters aren't all that bad . . . relatively speakin'."

"I'll keep that in mind, Mike."

Prophet mounted his horse and held the reins tight as the stage started away from the station, Clatsop yelling and cracking the blacksnake over the horses' backs, the dog nipping at the dust-dripping wheels.

"Good *riddance!*" Mrs. Phelps called to Prophet, poking her blunt face out the window.

When the stage was gone, Prophet saw the girl standing beside the Appaloosa. She held her carpetbag in both hands and was regarding him with bald disdain. He didn't blame her. He wished he would have left her alone. It was too late for that now, however. They were both in too deep—had too many men after them—to back out now.

"Well . . . we'd better ride," he said tiredly.

She lowered her gaze to her dress, then looped the handles of her bag over the Appaloosa's saddle. Bending down, she lifted the hem of her dress and tore a slit up to her thigh. When she was finished, she climbed into the saddle with an ease Prophet found surprising for a showgirl.

She must have noticed his appraisal. "Oh, my father

kept horses, and I rode all the time!" she grouched, brows furrowed with disdain. "Which way?"

"This way," he said, reining the speckle-gray south.

They rode single-file down the stage road for about a hundred yards. Then, by a stand of sun-dappled cotton-woods, Prophet abruptly turned his horse off the trail and headed east.

It was a big country they rode through, following game trails through hogbacks and sandstone buttes, cedar-studded rimrocks rising around them, sudden walls shutting out the horizon. They traced the folds in the hills, one fold after another. The sky was a vast, blue bowl. Hawks hunted the brush and trees lining water-courses, giving their shrill cries. Prairie dogs chortled.

The sun hot on her neck, Lola rode behind Prophet, her anger simmering deep inside her. She was too tired and discouraged to give voice to it now. She'd wanted to find a saddled horse on which she could escape this insane, brutish man . . . this Lou Prophet . . . but none had been available when she could have used it to escape. Besides, she'd been too exhausted to make a run for it, anyway.

So now she found herself having escaped death once again—by a very narrow margin—and following this madman horseback through the vast northwestern wil-derness, heading cross-country to Johnson City. She couldn't understand why he wouldn't release her. Didn't he see there was no way Billy Brown would let them live?

Some men were as stubborn as fate, and this Mr. Prophet was definitely one of those. After they'd camped for the night and Prophet was asleep, she'd take one of the horses and get away from the fool once and for all, before he got them both killed. She'd give him the slip if she first had to knock him in the head with a stone.

They'd traveled about forty-five minutes when Prophet reined up suddenly and jerked his gaze southward. Lola halted her horse, as well.

"What is it?"

"Did you hear something?"

She frowned. "No."

"I thought I heard gun shots."

"Great! Just great! They've followed us!"

"Shh."

"Don't shush me—"

His sharp look silenced her. He cast a look south again, squinting his eyes, straining his ears. He heard it again. Muffled gunfire. And that smudge above the butte about two hundred yards away . . . was that . . . ?

Sure enough . . . it was smoke.

The hair on the back of Prophet's neck bristled. It could very well be the stage road over there.

"You wait here," he ordered the girl, knowing full well she'd probably run. He couldn't worry about that now. If the smoke and gunfire were what he thought they were, he had a far bigger problem on his hands.

He gigged the horse into a ground-eating gallop, rising and falling over the rolling tablelands. He crested the saddle of a low butte and reined the speckle-gray to a skidding halt. Tossing his gaze to the flower-speckled prairie beneath him, he saw what he'd hoped he wouldn't:

The stage, fire licking up around the wheels, black smoke billowing into the sky.

Something moved along the stage road, right of the stage. Prophet turned his head to see four horseback riders galloping north, kicking up dust, their dusters flapping open, the sun winking off the hardware on their hips and protruding from their saddle boots.

Prophet clamped his jaws together and drew his lips

away from his teeth. "You goddamn sons of bitches!" he breathed, spurring his horse down the saddle, its front hooves digging deep into the sandy, rocky ground. When the terrain leveled once more, the horse sprang off its hind legs and stretched out in a hell-for-leather gallop, blowing hard, lather stringing off its lips.

Prophet approached the stage, dismounting as the horse skidded to a stop. He dropped the reins and hit the ground on the run. He'd run only five or six strides before he stopped suddenly, raising his arms against the heat of the thundering flames consuming the overturned carriage like so much scrap wood heaved on a bonfire. There was hardly a square foot of the red carriage housing not pocked with bullet holes.

The sons of bitches, whoever they were, had filled the stage with lead, no doubt killing everyone inside, then run it down and set it on fire. All the horses were dead— lifeless hairy humps strewn about the traces and shafts, blood leaking from the bullet wounds in their hides.

Prophet turned, looking around for Clatsop. He didn't see the jehu, however, until he'd walked a hundred yards north along the stage road. Then he found the man face-down in a sagebrush, Clatsop's body riddled with bullets, blood leaking through the holes in his cotton shirt and cowhide vest like a sieve.

Prophet hunkered down on his haunches and turned the man over, put a finger to the leathery neck. There was no pulse. He listened to the heart, but there was nothing there, either. What the hell was he expecting? There was more blood than unsoiled cloth on the man.

He'd just hoped . . . what? That he hadn't gotten *everyone* aboard the stage killed? His head throbbed and he lowered it, dislodging his hat and rubbing a heavy hand through his hair. Mrs. Phelps . . . her boy . . . the old miner . . .

All were dead because he'd insisted on taking the girl to the hearing in Johnson City.

He knelt there, head in his hands, as close to vomiting as he'd come since the war. His chest was heavy, and a lump burned in his throat. Every vein in his body throbbed with outrage and horror.

As he lifted his head to regard the burning stage wavering behind the flames and hot air, the enormity of his dilemma hit him full force. *What the hell you going to do now, Prophet?*

Finally, he replaced the hat on his head and staggered to his feet, looking down at Clatsop. He licked his lips and shook his head, wincing. "I'd like to give you a proper burial, ole boy, but there's no time."

Stiffly, he walked back to his horse, which had shied a good distance from the burning stage and the smell of its dead brethren, and was cropping grass in a hollow. Prophet mounted and rode back where he'd left the girl, surprised to find her there. She studied him worriedly as he rode up.

"What is it?" she asked, standing and holding her horse's reins. She could tell by the look on his face it wasn't good.

"The stage," he said grimly, not looking at her. His face was expressionless. "Mount up. We have to get the hell out of here."

He knew that whoever had attacked the stage had discovered, too late for the other passengers, that Prophet and Miss Diamond were not aboard. That's why they were racing northward, hoping to cut Prophet's trail. Prophet figured they'd do so within the hour.

"They're . . . all . . . dead?" the girl asked him. She hadn't run while Prophet was gone, because she, too, had sensed the stage had been attacked and had wanted to know the outcome.

Prophet sighed and nodded, looking off. "Mount up."

Her face was white, but her eyes were sharp. "You're quite the piece of work, Prophet."

"Mount up!" he raged, his head reeling. If only he'd stayed in Henry's Crossing. But he hadn't. He'd taken money for a job, and it was a job he was going to finish.

She did as he ordered, and they gigged their horses off at a trot.

They rode hard, stopping only to rest and water their mounts. Prophet found jerky in the saddlebags draped over the back of Lola's Appaloosa, and they ate while they rode. They did not converse; the troubled silence hanging between them was almost palpable. Prophet could feel the girl's loathing, but it was nothing compared to the resentment he felt for himself.

He saw nothing of those pursuing them until, toward day's end, he rode to the top of a low rimrock and trained his spyglass on their backtrail. There, just beyond the last divide, he saw the light spray of dust tinted orange by the falling sun. It could have been dust kicked up by drovers, as this was cow country, but something told Prophet it was not.

Reducing the spyglass and returning it to his saddlebags, he caught up with the girl, and they spurred their horses into a canter. They rode through a canyon that let out on a creek bottom. They followed the creek into another, shallower canyon rimmed with junipers. By midday they'd crossed a shelf of low, grassy hills and stopped to rest and water their horses along a spring bubbling among the glacial rubble of boulders.

It was a country so huge and varied it was hard to believe it was all of one territory, under a sky scalloped with high, serried clouds. Wherever they looked they saw deer and antelope. Sign of cougar, fox, and lion were at every turn in their trail. Since Prophet hadn't eaten breakfast, he was hungry and believed the girl must be as well. But he couldn't dare a shot at game out here, with the firebrands behind them.

When the horses were watered and Prophet had smoked a cigarette, he and the girl sitting a good ways apart, not saying a word, they mounted again and followed an old buffalo trail over a bench and through a prairie. Blond grass ruffled in the wind. Cloud shadows flickered sunlight.

Toward the end of the day they endured a short rain, hunkered low in their saddles. The purple clouds rolled over them, and the sun came out, even brighter than before.

The sun was nearly down before Prophet stopped for the night in an ancient riverbed. He walked the high points around the camp, scouting their backtrail. Seeing no sign of those following, he thought it was safe to shoot a rabbit, so he did so—a big jack that weighed close to ten pounds.

He roasted the jack over the fire and brewed coffee in the pot he found in the girl's saddlebags. He and the girl ate hungrily, again sharing no words. The girl didn't even look at him.

When they'd finished eating, it was dark, the sky awash with stars. Prophet checked on the horses he'd staked in a patch of green grass, then returned to the fire. The girl had already rolled up in her blanket and rested her head on her saddle, sound asleep.

Prophet sat up for an hour, looking into the darkness beyond the fire, watching and listening. He smoked several cigarettes as he sipped his coffee. Finally, he took apart his revolver, setting the parts on a bandanna spread out beside him. He cleaned and oiled the parts, snapped them back together, and did the same to his rifle and sawed-off eight-gauge.

He had a feeling he was going to be in dire need of each weapon soon, and he wanted to make sure each functioned properly.

Tired as he was, it took him over an hour to fall asleep, the stage burning behind his eyelids. He'd just sailed off when something woke him. His eyes opened. The girl stood over him holding a large stone above her head. She glared down at him.

He rolled sideways, the rock grazing his right shoulder as it careened out of the girl's hands. He scissored his legs, kicking the girl's feet out from under her. She fell with an angry scream.

"Ow! Goddamn, you son of a bitch!"

Prophet stood, grabbed her arm, and dragged her back to her saddle. He retrieved the lariat from his own saddle, tied her wrists together as she squirmed, kicked, and cursed—and tied her wrists to the horn of the saddle she'd been sleeping on.

"There you go," he said, heading back to his own bed. "Sleep tight."

Gradually, her cries diminished, and they both slept.

13

OWEN MCCREEDY WAS sitting at his desk in the jailhouse in Johnson City, smoking a thin cigar and going over his court docket. He'd just turned a page of the big book when he heard a yell from the cell block.

The sheriff set his cigar in the ashtray, stood, and walked to the door leading into the cell block. He opened the door and yelled, "I'm not getting you any more tobacco, Brown. You've smoked a whole bag since yesterday."

"Look at the goddamn clock," came the shout from the cell. "It's supper time!"

"So it is," McCreedy said without interest.

"I want my supper, goddamnit! I got rights!"

"I'll fetch your supper when I'm goddamn ready to fetch it."

Billy Brown's voice came low and tight with emotion. "Why don't you come back here, McCreedy? Why don't you open up this door, so you and I can go at it the way we really want? Huh? Why don't you do that?"

Knees quaking with rage, McCreedy walked down the short hall between the four cells, stopping at the last cell on the left. Billy Brown stood with his hands gripping the iron bars, his bristly cheeks spread wide with a grin. His blue eyes flashed demonically. "There you go. Now just open the door and step in here, and you and me, we'll settle this thing once and for all."

He was about two inches shorter than McCreedy, but the sheriff figured Brown outweighed him by at least twenty pounds.

"If I stepped in there, you'd never walk out. Ever."

Brown chuckled. "You think so? Why don't you try it? Come on, open the door."

McCreedy stared at the man between the bars. His face was impassive, but he hated the stout, ham-fisted Irishman more than he'd ever hated anyone. Brown was a blight on the town—McCreedy's town. As long as Brown was in business, Johnson City would not flourish the way it should . . . peaceably, drawing civilized, honest citizens and their families. As long as Billy Brown was in business, McCreedy would continue to be the laughing-stock Brown thumbed his nose at, and Johnson City would be a hotbed of vice and underhanded business dealings, driving the honest folks out and replacing them with more no-accounts like Brown himself.

At the moment, however, what bothered McCreedy more was knowing that if he opened Brown's cell door and took Brown's bait, Brown would beat him senseless. Brown had been a street fighter who'd made his way with his fists. McCreedy had been a farmboy from Nebraska, who'd come to Montana when he was seventeen, to punch cows. He'd been in his share of fistfights but nothing like those that had forged Billy Brown.

McCreedy hated himself for it, but he was afraid of Brown. And what really burned him was that Brown knew it. Brown knew he wouldn't open the cell door and accept the challenge. Brown knew he was afraid, and the challenge was just more of the criminal's attempts at intimidation, which he'd honed on the town's other saloon owners, whose earnings he regularly skimmed.

"You think so, do you, Owen?" Brown taunted, shadowboxing, fading this way and that. "Well, come on, then—open the door."

McCreedy stared at him coolly, trying not to look intimidated, trying not to show his insecurities and his anger. What he wanted to do more than anything was draw the Colt on his hip and shoot Billy Brown through his forehead. The problem was, McCreedy was an honest, law-abiding man, which was why the majority of Johnson City's citizens had elected him sheriff two years ago. If he shot Brown, he'd be no better than Brown. He'd be letting the honest citizens down.

"I'd love to tussle with you, Billy," McCreedy said casually, "but that isn't how I do my job."

With that he walked slowly back toward his office, feeling a flush prickle around his neck.

"Yeah, I know how you do your job, you weak-kneed tinhorn!" Brown shouted after him. "You cower behind your badge! Now bring me my supper, goddamnit!"

McCreedy walked back to his desk and sat down in his creaky chair. He picked up his cigar and puffed away, trying to calm his nerves and distract himself, but it was no use. He knew he should go over to the Excelsior and get Brown's supper. Mrs. Dornan would probably have it dished up and waiting for McCreedy, and as much as McCreedy wanted to keep Brown waiting, he couldn't do that to Eunice Dornan.

"All right, goddamnit," he grouched, stubbing out his cigar in the ashtray.

Standing, he retrieved his hat off the coat tree, and walked out the door. He headed across the street through the spare, late-day traffic. At the busy Excelsior, he found Mrs. Dornan in the kitchen, ladling soup into bowls. Her husband, Johnny Dornan, was manning the big cast-iron range, on which several steaks sizzled and potatoes sat in warming racks. A five-gallon kettle of green beans simmered, sending steam to the rafters.

"I'm here for my prisoner's supper, Eunice," McCreedy said, letting the louvered doors swing shut behind him.

"In a minute, Owen," Mrs. Dornan said, turning toward him with a tray of bowls. "It got so busy today, I plum forgot." She disappeared through the louvered doors, where a dozen or so businessmen, miners, and railroad surveyors were awaiting their meals. Their talk was loud and boisterous, and the cigar and cigarette smoke was thick.

"No hurry," Owen called after her.

Flipping steaks, Johnny Dornan glanced at him. He was tall and spare, with thinning brown hair and a large birthmark on his long neck. His apron was splashed with blood and grease. "Still got ole Billy Brown locked up over there, eh, Owen?"

"Of course, I do, Johnny. What'd you think—I set him loose on good behavior?" Billy Brown had gotten to be a touchy subject for McCreedy, since almost everyone he knew thought he was a fool for tangling with the man. He knew they were only worried about his safety, but he could have used a little encouragement.

"Just seems like a mighty big chunk to chew, if you ask me," Johnny said, shaking his head slowly.

Mrs. Dornan walked through the doors and set down her tray. Moving quickly, she retrieved a plate from a high stack by the range. "Put a steak on that for Billy, Johnny," she said.

"How's he like his steaks, Owen?" Johnny asked.

"I don't care, but probably rare," McCreedy said dryly.

"There, that should do it," Johnny said, dropping a steak on the plate.

Mrs. Dornan forked a potato beside the steak, added a spoonful of green beans, and covered it all with a napkin. Handing the plate to McCreedy, she said, "If you'd only let me add a good dose of strychnine, Owen, your job would be finished."

"Now, now, Eunice."

"How's Alice—have you seen her?"

McCreedy shook his head, a tired, drawn look stealing over his features. "No—I can't leave the jail unattended. Besides, someone might follow me."

Eunice Dornan acquired a pained look, shaking her head and squinting her eyes. The hair on her forehead was slick with perspiration. "Are you sure you want to do this, Owen?"

"It's not a choice for me, Eunice. I have him on suspicion of murder. What do you want me to do, turn him loose because I'm afraid one of his gunslicks is going to shoot me in the back?"

"Yes!"

"I can't do that, Eunice."

"I'm so afraid for you, Owen. I've heard talk in here, late at night, among his men. They're so . . . brash! The things they say about you, what they'd like to do to keep him from going to trial—"

"They won't do anything, Eunice. They know that if they did they'd have U.S. marshals in here in a heartbeat." Not confident that were true—the nearest marshal was nearly two hundred miles away—he turned for the door. "Well, I'd better get this to my prisoner."

She stopped him with a hand on his shoulder. "You be careful, Owen. You and Alice . . . you're such good people."

He forced a smile, inwardly resenting her apparent lack of confidence in his abilities. "Thanks, Eunice."

"See ya, Owen," Johnny called after him.

On his way through the dining area, faces turned his way, and he saw three distinct expressions: admiration, worry, and disdain. Outside he was met with more disdain as a gun fired to his right, so loudly it numbed his ears and set them ringing. He jumped, dropping the plate and reaching for the Colt Army on his hip.

"It's all right, Sheriff—I think I got him," said a man to his right, walking toward him on the boardwalk.

It was one of Billy Brown's firebrands—a tall man in a cream duster, checked shirt, and wool vest, a pair of matched Colts tied low on his thighs. He grinned maliciously. "A rattlesnake slinking around under the boardwalk, ready to poke his head through a knot and bite you."

McCreedy looked down at the fresh bullet hole in the board about a foot wide of his right foot. He had his hand on his revolver's grips, but he had not drawn the gun. Looking around, he saw four more of Brown's firebrands facing him around the street and on the boardwalks, heads tilted rakishly, mouths stretching grins.

"The only snakes I see are you and them," McCreedy growled, aware of the restaurant's open door behind him, and the faces crowded in the doorway.

Citizens up and down the street had stopped to see what the gunfire was about, and they were watching McCreedy expectantly, wondering what he would do. His face was flushed with anger, but he knew there was no action he could take. He felt weak and cornered, like a rabid coon trapped by dogs in a woodshed.

The firebrand who'd shot into the boardwalk shook his head mockingly. "No, I seen him ... a snake about to poke his head through a knot. Ain't it somethin', though—all the ways a man can die?"

McCreedy glowered at the man, wanting to shoot him, knowing he wouldn't. "Why don't you just come out and say what you mean?"

"That's all I mean, Sheriff. Ain't it awful to think about—all the ways there is to get killed around here?" With that, the man sauntered off the boardwalk, crossed the street, and pushed through the louvered doors of a saloon. Slowly, the other men followed him, several mockingly tipping their hats at the sheriff.

McCreedy stood on the boardwalk. Several townsmen stood around watching him.

"Why don't you just go on about your business!" he grouched.

Then he kicked the overturned plate aside, damned if he'd get another for Billy Brown, and headed back to the jail. He slammed the door and stood with his back to it. He tried to quell the shaking in his knees to no avail.

He hoped Prophet got here before Brown's men made good on their threat.

14

PROPHET WOKE BEFORE dawn. He looked around, listening to the first birds, noting the fading stars, then stretched and rolled his blanket. He removed his knife from his belt sheath and walked over to the girl. She stirred as he cut the ropes tethering her wrists to her saddle horn.

"I hate you," she said without heat. She stared at him dully, sleep-mussed hair in her eyes. "I really hate you."

"I know that. And to tell you the truth, I don't blame you." He sheathed the knife. "But I have a job to do, and I'm going to do it."

"I'm an actress, goddamnit," she said through a sob. "I worked with some of the best actors in the East. Now . . . look where I am." She lifted her outraged eyes to his. "Being carted through the wilderness like some . . . some . . . fatted calf to the slaughter."

"I know you're an actress, and I know these are rather humbling circumstances, but—"

"Oh, I know—*you've got a job to do!*"

He squatted down beside her. She was rubbing the circulation back into her wrists. "Aren't you tired of running?"

She only looked at him through puffy, teary eyes.

He continued, "That's what you've been doing, isn't it? Runnin' from this Billy Brown, because you saw what he did and you know if he ever catches you, he'll kill you."

"Of course I'm running. Who wouldn't run from him?"

"Well, how long you going to run?" Prophet asked her.

He stood when he saw she wasn't going to respond. "I'll saddle the horses. We'll ride for an hour or so before breakfast. That way we'll know if they're behind us or not."

He grabbed the bridles and started away, then stopped and faced her again. "If you try to run out on me again, I'll catch you, and I'll leave you tied all day to your saddle."

He wheeled and walked out to where the horses were tied in the grass. When he had them bridled, he led them into the camp. As he finished saddling the Appaloosa, the girl returned from tending nature and washing at the spring, and knelt to roll her blanket. She tied the ends and stood. Prophet took the blanket roll, tied it behind her saddle, and helped her mount.

"How much farther?" she said.

"Two-, three-day ride . . . if we don't get held up, that is."

"How long do we have?"

"Five days starting day before yesterday."

"They're going to let him go after the fifth day?"

"That's what I understand," Prophet said, mounting the speckle-gray.

"I hope they let him go."

Prophet shook his head and led off at a walk. "You sure must like running."

They followed the riverbed for a quarter mile, then traced a game trail onto a hilly prairie pocked with low, chalky buttes and yucca. It was a low, dry area, and Prophet knew they were getting close to the badlands they would have to traverse—about fifteen miles of deep canyons carved by prehistoric rivers and creeks. There would be little water, Prophet knew, having heard stories of men who'd traversed the area. He had never done so himself, preferring to take the extra day or two to circumvent the rough country by trails.

It was a deep-cut country, hard to traverse, but those behind them would have trouble traversing it, as well. Prophet thought he might even be able to hold up and lure them into his rifle sights, pick them off one at a time. . . .

About an hour after they'd started riding, Prophet motioned the girl to stop. Reining his horse northward, he gigged the animal halfway up a butte and dismounted. The sun was up, hitting the layered terrain at a slant, drawing deep shadows relieved by swaths of golden, dew-dappled sun.

After surveying the country and deciding those following—if they were still following—were not close, he mounted the speckle-gray and rode back down to the girl.

"I think it's safe to stop here for a bite," he said.

"What's there to eat?" she asked.

"Rabbit from last night."

Prophet dismounted and fished around in his saddle-bags, producing a red bandanna in which he'd tied the leftovers. He held up the pouch, offered a smile, walked over to a rock, and sat down. He hiked a boot on a knee.

"It's old," she said, making no move to dismount.

"Only a few hours," Prophet replied, chewing a chunk of the meat. "Won't hurt ye."

"Our neighbor in New York got sick eating old meat."

"You from New York?"

"That's what I just said, didn't I?"

He glanced at her wryly. "All the girls in New York have as much charm as you?"

She wrinkled her nose. "Only those hauled kicking and screaming by bounty hunters to Billy Brown." She swung her leg over the Appaloosa's rump, dismounting. "Here . . . give me a chunk of that. Might as well die by spoiled meat as a bullet."

He gave her the pouch and wiped his greasy hands on his jeans. "Now you're talkin'."

He got up, stretched his back and shoulder, and walked around. She sat on the rock, eating the rabbit, and watched him.

He was a big, sun-seared hombre, not unlike a lot of other men she had met on the frontier. Big, dirty, crude, good with his weapons and animals—he couldn't have been much less different from her than night was from day, but even after all the pain he'd caused her—was causing her—she found that she could not totally hate him. True, she'd tried to put him out with a rock last night, but only because she'd been afraid for her life and had wanted to run.

But there was something about him that she almost found herself admiring. His cunning and directness? The way he always averted his eyes—very gentlemanly—from the slit she'd torn in her dress? The way he also never made her feel threatened sexually, as a woman could out here, alone with a man of his obviously ignoble breeding?

She suspected she approved of all those things about him. But there were things she hated about him, too.

His arrogance for one. And his single-mindedness. It was as though when he got headed in one direction, it would take a veritable act of God to sway him, if indeed he could be swayed. Lola thought he probably couldn't. The problem was, he was simple. When someone told him to do something, and gave him money to do it, he simply did it. No questions asked. Forget any others who might get hurt in the process.

And there had been plenty of others hurt thus far. And there would most likely be more. . . .

Simple men like Prophet were no doubt invaluable in the building of the West, just like soldiers were invaluable in waging war. Lola just wished she had not crossed paths with such a man.

Now that she had, and now that they were out here in the middle of nowhere, she didn't know what she was going to do. Running seemed out of the question. She could kill Prophet with the gun strapped to her leg, but then she'd be out here alone, and she had no idea where she could go to find safety. She'd probably starve to death, if Brown's men didn't find her first. Or Indians.

It looked as though, for the moment at least, she was stuck with the uncouth Prophet. Unless she could persuade him that taking her to Johnson City meant certain death for them both. . . .

They'd been riding for fifteen minutes when she made her move.

"You want to know what happened?"

Prophet rode ahead of her, moving lightly with his horse, swinging his head this way and that as he surveyed the terrain around them.

"What's that?"

"Back in Johnson City. You want to know what I saw?"

"I don't know—is it going to frighten me?"

She'd started to respond seriously when she saw his head turn and saw the wry expression creasing his ruddy cheeks. She stopped herself and scowled, realizing she was being teased. She went ahead with the story, anyway.

"Billy Brown killed a saloon owner in Johnson City—the owner of the saloon where my troupe was staying. And I saw it happen." She paused, frowning, eyes acquiring a haunted cast as she remembered. "That night I went downstairs for some water and heard a commotion. I cracked a back-room door just in time to see Billy Brown slit Hoyt Farley's throat with a knife."

She watched Prophet's sweat-stained back expectantly as they rode. Much to her annoyance, he didn't say anything for nearly a minute. "What was it about?"

She shrugged. "Who knows? Billy Brown has a stranglehold on the town. What matters is that he did do it, and I saw it with my own eyes."

"And he saw you?"

She nodded. "I gasped when I saw the knife. . . . They heard me—him and the two men with him. I ran out the back and they chased me, but it was dark and I hid in a root cellar until morning. I knew I couldn't go back to my troupe. They'd be laying for me. So I went to another troupe I knew was leaving town that morning, and Dan Walthrop signed me on."

"How did Brown get caught?"

"I don't know. I heard shooting and yelling behind me, but I didn't stop to check it out. Even if someone saw him and his men chase me out of the saloon, there's nothing the sheriff could do about it. Like I said, Billy Brown has a stranglehold on the town. His enemies have a way of disappearing and turning up dead in trash heaps. I was only in town four nights, but Billy Brown was the main topic of conversation everywhere I went. Whispered conversation, that is. I even heard a child threatened in the mercantile with 'You be good or Billy Brown will get you.' "

She shuddered, and it was not entirely staged. She watched Prophet, gauging his reaction. "It was awful . . . just awful."

Prophet sighed. "Sounds to me like Billy Brown needs to be taken down a notch."

"I doubt there's anyone in the territory who can do that, Mr. Prophet. And anyone who tries is going to end up dead."

He turned around in his saddle to regard her slyly. "Like me?"

"If you intend to tangle with him, yes. And escorting me to Johnson City is definitely tangling with him."

Prophet slowed his horse so Miss Diamond's could catch up. When it did, they rode stirrup to stirrup along the cutbank of a wide creek bed.

"I don't only intend to escort you to Johnson City, Miss Diamond. I intend to have a little chat with the man. I don't much appreciate having gunmen sicced on me. Never have, never will."

She laughed without mirth, lifting her head. "You're a brave man, Mr. Prophet. I'm impressed. You're also a dead man. Very dead. Do you hear? *Dead!*"

"It sounds like my ole pal Owen McCreedy has his hands tied, on account of him wearin' a badge and all," the bounty hunter continued, as though he hadn't heard her. "Well, my hands aren't tied by any badge." He flashed her a shrewd smile.

Her face became rigid, and her eyes blazed as she regarded him directly. Once again she was reminded that the man was too stupid to know fear. His reckless disregard for his own safety would get them both killed. "Why, you moron! You—!"

The unmistakable bark of a rifle cut her off. She gave a scream and tumbled against Prophet, who grabbed her under both arms. He saw where the bullet had grazed her shoulder, tearing her dress. Awkwardly, both horses shuffling with fright, Prophet pulled her out of her saddle, then eased her to the ground. As another rifle barked in the north, he swung out of the leather and grabbed the girl's good arm.

"Come on—down the bank!" he yelled, drawing his revolver and firing blindly northward, hoping to put the shooters on the defensive long enough for him and the girl to gain shelter behind the cutbank.

As they jumped down the bank, sliding in the loose clay, he heard their horses gallop away, and he hoped they ran beyond rifle range. All he needed was for one or both of the horses to go down. That would fix him and the girl good.

Reprimanding himself for getting careless and not keeping an eye on their surroundings, leading them into an ambush, he released the girl, removed his hat, and gentled a look over the lip of the cutbank. About a hundred yards away, a horse stood ground-hitched near a grassy knoll. On the knoll, Prophet could make out a prone gunman aiming a rifle.

Spotting movement to the man's right, Prophet turned and saw three riders fanning out, as though to circle Prophet and the girl's position, but were in no hurry to get within range of Prophet's Peacemaker. They didn't have to be. If they surrounded Prophet, getting behind him in the creek bed, they could fling rifle slugs from a hundred yards away and hit their targets quite effectively. Like ducks in a shooting gallery.

The bounty hunter's thoughts flickered with doubt. Maybe he should have set the girl on her way, after all. Maybe these men really were too much for him.

Damn! If he'd only had time to grab his Winchester from his saddle boot! Still . . . it was four against one, and the men were moving to acquire the positions Prophet had feared.

He looked around. There was no cover—no shrubs or boulders—anywhere near. The only cover within a hundred yards was the brush tracing the very center of the creek bed, beyond the sand, gravel, and driftwood that accumulated when the creek swelled each spring and was left high and dry when the water retreated.

The girl sobbed as she clutched her shoulder. Prophet turned to her. "How bad is it?"

She lifted her face, flushed with anger. "What does it look like? They shot me, you—!"

"It's just a burn. You can make it."

"Where?"

"There."

She followed his pointing finger to the cattails and saw grass behind them. Not having seen the three men surrounding them, she couldn't fathom what Prophet was up to. He had no time to explain.

"Huh?" she said, wrinkling up her face.

He grabbed her arm and jerked her to her feet. "Come on!"

They hadn't run ten yards before the lead started to fly like lightning from Zeus.

15

THE SLUGS POCKED the ground around them, spanging off rocks with shrill, echoing rings. The three horsemen had dismounted when they saw Prophet and the girl heading for the weeds. Trying to head them off, they knelt and cut loose with their rifles.

It was a barrage like Prophet hadn't experienced since he and his buddy, Trav Davis, were bushwacked by a small Union patrol when they'd lit out from a barn in which they'd spent the night and where Prophet had tended Trav's wounds inflicted by an exploding cannon ball.

Trav had lasted only another day, dying in Prophet's arms before the next moon was up. Prophet wasn't sure he and the girl would make it, either, as close as those slugs were humming around their tender flesh.

"Run, run, run!" Prophet shouted as a slug buzzed viciously past his ear.

They were halfway to the weeds, nearly breaking their ankles on the small rocks of the creek bed, nearly tripping over driftwood and a bison's bleached carcass, when Prophet took a bullet in his calf. It felt like the nip of a large horsefly, and he forced himself to ignore it until that foot gave and he fell to one knee.

"No! Keep going!" he raged when the girl stopped and turned to him, terrified.

She did as he'd told her, and he pushed back on both feet, fighting the pain of the bullet in his calf, and ran in spite of the fire shooting up past his knee and into his thigh.

He followed the girl deep into the weeds, until they came to the brackish, foul-smelling water. It was black as molasses and barely moving. Something scratched in a heavy cattail patch. Nervy from the barrage, Prophet gave a start. Only a small beaver or muskrat, he knew. Maybe a duck that hadn't flown when the gunfire had started.

"Oh, my god! Oh, my god!" the girl cried, staring at the blood welling out of Prophet's calf, soaking his jeans. She cupped her hands to her face. He knew she wasn't worried so much about him as about what she'd do if she were suddenly alone out here.

"Just a scratch," Prophet said, trying for calm in both himself and her. "Stay low."

They were on their knees, the tops of the cattails and saw grass waving a good three feet above their heads. Prophet held his Peacemaker in his right hand. He peered through the weeds, lifting his head slightly for a better look. When the breeze parted the weeds, he saw the three horsemen walking this way. They'd left their horses behind and were holding their rifles before them in both hands.

Turning northward, he saw the fourth gunman—the

man who'd fired at them from the knoll—hunkered down on his haunches atop the cutbank, not far from where Prophet and the girl had been. Prophet recognized the Big Fifty in his arms—a Sharp's buffalo gun accurate up to seven hundred yards. The sun winked off the brass breech and butt plate. Prophet was just glad the shooter wasn't as accurate as the rifle, or it would've been taps for the girl.

"You boys flush 'em and I'll shoot 'em!" the man with the Big Fifty called, his voice muffled by distance.

"Why don't you come down here and flush 'em?" one of the others returned. "You can't hit anything with that cannon anyways."

The man with the buffalo gun didn't say anything, but Prophet saw him raise the gun to his shoulder, evidently drawing a bead on the man who'd mouthed off at him. That was enough to silence the others while they kicked around in the weeds, spread about ten paces apart, trying to flush Prophet and the girl like deer. They'd either shoot them themselves or feed them to the Sharp's.

Prophet's chest and throat filled with bile. He turned to the girl kneeling beside him, who clutched her bloody left shoulder with her right hand and stared wide-eyed through the weeds, her face blanched with fear. There was no longer any anger there. Only fear. She suddenly looked so girlish and innocent that Prophet felt sorry for her. He felt like even more of a heel than he had before.

If it wasn't for him, she might still be running, but she'd at least be safe. . . .

He turned back toward the faint sounds of the three gunmen walking through the weeds along the creek, moving steadily this way. He didn't dare lift his head very high, for the man with the Big Fifty might see him and alert the others . . . or go ahead and take it off with his buffalo gun.

Damn, what a mess!

He turned and considered the water. He and the girl could try to wade across the creek and hide on the other side, but the three gunmen were approaching too quickly. Prophet could hear their movements growing louder— could even hear their harsh breathing and occasional throat clearings. They'd probably hear Prophet and the girl in the water, and really pin them down.

No . . . they'd have to stay put and fight it out. There was no other way.

Prophet looked at the girl. Her eyes slid up to meet his. He tried to steel her with a look, and she seemed to understand. To his surprise—maybe she had more sand than he'd given her credit for—a faint smile nipped at the very corners of her lips. Then her gaze returned to the direction from which the three gunmen were approaching.

"That's about where they went into the weeds!" the man with the Big Fifty called from atop the cutbank. "Be careful."

None of the others replied, but Prophet could tell from the sudden silence that they'd stopped in their tracks. Prophet's heart beat harshly against his sternum, and his mouth went dry. He strained his ears to listen—only the faint scratching of the breeze-bending weeds, the faint sucking of the creek. On the bank across the water, a prairie dog chortled.

"You in here, friend?" one of the men called, tentative, as though his own pulse were racing.

Prophet figured he was about thirty feet away. The bounty hunter slowly thumbed back the hammer of his forty-five. When it locked, he left his thumb on it, taking an unconscious comfort in the grooved grip. He sensed the girl tense, heard her give a barely audible gasp. But something told him she wouldn't break down and give them away. He didn't try to shush her with a look.

There was a faint rustling of weeds, as if the man closest to him took another step or two forward. The man cleared his throat. "Why don't you send the girl out, friend? We'll let you live."

More rustling, and the man's hatted head came into view through the bending weed tips. Prophet lowered his own head while lifting his chin, feeling a dull pain in the back of his neck. His calf throbbed metronomically.

"Come on, friend, be reasonable," the man continued. "What's ole McCreedy payin' you, anyway? Can't be enough for your life."

There was a long, breeze-brushed pause. More rustling, the snap of a stout weed under a boot.

"Sure enough, friend. We'll let you go—scot-free," the man said, his voice growing louder as he approached. He was only about ten yards away and facing just north of Prophet and the girl.

Prophet's heart hammered as the man swung his head toward him. The man's eyes grew large as they found Prophet. He started lifting his rifle, but he was too late. Prophet jumped to his feet, ignoring the pain in his right leg, and shot the man through the chest. The man went over backwards, discharging his rifle in the air and giving a clipped scream.

Prophet knew the other two men and probably the man with the Big Fifty were bearing down on him, but he didn't have time to find out which was bearing down on him fastest. He had to pick one and shoot, and to that end he wheeled to his left. About thirty yards away, another man already had his rifle to his shoulder. Prophet fired a quarter second before the rifle sprouted smoke and flames. Dropping the rifle, the man grabbed his neck, twisted, stumbled backwards, and fell without a sound.

Before he hit the ground, Prophet turned slightly right

and saw the third gunman running toward him through
the weeds. He was about forty yards away and closing,
yelling something unintelligible, raising his rifle as the
wind tore his cream Stetson from his head, revealing a
thatch of wavy, chestnut hair.

Prophet knew he couldn't get off a shot before the man
running toward him did, so he dove forward just as he
heard the rifle bark. The weeds were too high—he
couldn't see through them—but he fired through them,
anyway, hoping for a lucky shot. Then, knowing that his
chances of having hit the man were slim, and also knowing the man would probably fire at the spot where he'd
seen Prophet hit the ground, he rolled to his left.

Just as he'd suspected, the man fired a barrage of bullets where Prophet had landed, the slugs whistling and
crackling through the weeds and tearing into the spongy
ground with decisive thumps. As the man fired, the slugs
grew closer and closer to Prophet, for the gunman was
keying on the weeds Prophet bent as he rolled. To top it
all off, the fourth man was cutting loose with the Big
Fifty, the fifty-caliber booms lifting boldly and horrifi-
cally above the wind.

Prophet knew he couldn't keep rolling forever, but he
also knew that when he stopped, he'd no doubt catch a
bullet. Then the shooting stopped, and Prophet, grunting
with fear and exertion, his breath rasping in and out of
his lungs, stopped rolling. He climbed to his feet, lifted
the Peacemaker to his shoulder, and aimed in the direction of the third rifleman.

But the man wasn't there. Prophet's heart increased its
pounding, and he jerked in a half-circle, searching for the
man while expecting a slug to tear through him at any
moment. Behind him, a gun cracked. Prophet jumped.
The small-caliber pistol cracked again as Prophet turned,
aiming the Peacemaker.

It was the girl, standing and holding her small, silver-plated revolver in both hands. She flicked back the trigger, scrunched up her face as she aimed down the barrel, then blinking and recoiling as she fired, the small gun jumping in her hands.

Looking northward, Prophet saw the man with the Big Fifty galloping away on his mouse-brown gelding with the single white sock. He'd mounted so quickly he hadn't had time to sheathe the buffalo gun, which dangled from his right hand.

The girl steadied the gun on him again, and fired. The man turned a look over his shoulder, the brim of his hat bending in the wind, then jerked back around, spurring his horse over a rise and out of sight.

Prophet stared flabbergasted at the girl, the Peacemaker falling to his side. Remembering the third gunman, he jerked back around, lifting the Peacemaker once again.

"I shot him," the girl said, turning to him.

Prophet walked cautiously forward and, sure enough, found the third gunman lying dead with a bullet through his forehead. He glanced back at the girl, surprised by her prowess with the thirty-two.

Prophet knelt down, removed the man's revolver from his holster, and picked up the man's rifle—a new-model Winchester, freshly cleaned and oiled.

"Is he dead?" the girl called.

Prophet turned and walked toward her. He nodded. "He's dead, all right. Where in hell did you get that thing, anyway?"

Her eyes were haunted as she stared at the bent grass where the dead man lay. "Brian Kildavies gave it to me."

"Who's Brian Kildavies?"

"A fine old actor I met in San Francisco. He was finally dying of a bullet wound he'd received in the war, and gave me the gun when he learned I was heading to the frontier. He said you never knew who you'd meet out there." She formed a crooked half-smile.

Prophet scratched his head, giving a befuddled look. "Well . . . that was some . . . good shootin', I reckon."

Her haunted eyes strayed to him slowly. "I never shot a man before." Her gaze grew fishy once more as she returned it to the matted weeds where the dead man lay.

"Could've fooled me," Prophet muttered. As he started limping away on his wounded leg, using his new rifle for a cane, he said, "We'd best track down our horses before that hombre with the Big Fifty comes back for more."

"Will he do that?" she asked.

"With the reward you have on you," Prophet said with a sigh, "you can bet your pantaloons he will."

16

ON HIS BAD leg and cursing with every step, Prophet tracked the horses down in a small box canyon. They were idly cropping grass, reins dangling around their feet.

He discovered that his own horse came to a whistle. The girl's horse, however, was more skittish, and Prophet had to run it down atop the speckle-gray, reaching out and grabbing the reins just before it broke into a gallop. He led the Appaloosa back to where the girl waited in the shade of a sandstone escarpment, bathing her wounded shoulder in the water that bubbled out of the rocks.

In spite of his painful calf, he knew a moment's arousal when he saw the skin the girl had exposed when she'd slipped the sleeve of her dress halfway down her arm, revealing a good bit of ample cleavage. The sensation was not at all welcome, and he was vaguely star-

tled and disgruntled that after all he'd been through—
after the bullet he'd taken in his calf—that a woman
needed only to reveal a little more skin than usual to
make his member stiffen.

He'd always known he was a rather simple mecha-
nism—plenty of women had told him so—but the current
revelation was all the more startling for his being in such
an otherwise foul mood.

Why the hell hadn't he stayed in Henry's Crossing and
drank himself stupid?

"Pack some mud on it and let's ride," he ordered. "You
can tend it more after sundown."

"It won't stop bleeding."

"Pack some mud on it, and that'll stop it. Let's go.
We don't have time for dawdlin'. If that polecat with the
Big Fifty follows like I think he's going to, you'll have
more holes than that one to worry about."

She turned to him sharply, red hair flying. "What are
you so goddamn mad about? You act like I'm the one
that got us ambushed!"

Prophet flushed as her barb hit home. He realized he'd
gotten careless back there but wasn't about to admit it to
her. "I said pack some mud on your shoulder, and mount
your goddamn horse!"

She grabbed up a handful of mud, laid it on the wound,
and stalked over to the Appaloosa idly cropping grass.
Grabbing the reins out of Prophet's hand, she turned a
look on him that would have sent Lucifer packing. "You
son of a bitch, Prophet!" Then she mounted with an angry huff.

Without looking at her, Prophet reined his horse
around and led out at a canter which he quickly stretched
into a gallop, ignoring the fire burning in his leg. They
had to eat some ground if they were going to reach Johnson City before Owen McCreedy set Billy Brown free,

and if they were going to stay ahead of that Big Fifty, as well.

They'd ridden for only a half hour before they came to the badlands, the cuts and gouges spreading out before them as far as the eye could see. Under the harsh, midday light, it was a menacing moonscape relieved here and there by tiny mesas and round-topped buttes slashed by the runoff of recent rains. It was a maze of sandy canyons in which the only green was a smattering of grass and sage in the lowest areas, and the spindly spikes of yucca.

In the hazy blue distance, two hawks hovered low over the canyons in their hunt for mice and rabbits—two black specks lazing on thermals, appearing nearly stationary.

Lola Diamond turned to Prophet with the angry, terrified expression that had become glued to her face over the past couple of days. "You're insane."

"It's shorter this way than by the stage road. And Brown's men—and whoever else is after us—will have a lot tougher time tracking us down there, too."

He spurred his horse toward a game trail winding into the canyon yawning below.

"Wait," she said. "I need a rest and so does my horse."

"No time" was his curt reply. He rode until he and his horse disappeared into the canyon.

"You son of a bitch," she muttered, hating his arrogance. He knew very well she wouldn't stay here alone, would have to follow him like a dog no matter how much she wanted to do otherwise.

She reined her own horse to the game trail, then closed her eyes as the animal took halting, mincing steps into the canyon. It was a steep descent, and halfway down the horse broke into a run, which it checked when it reached bottom.

It looked around as though wondering where to go. Lola did the same. All she saw before her was several sandy buttes with sage growing along their gravelly bases, each with a much-used game trail winding around its bulk.

Which trail had Prophet taken?

She called his name.

There was no response but the distant screech of a hunting hawk and the breeze playing in the bushes along the rim. The sun beat straight down upon her, so that her hat barely shaded her face. She knew a moment's concern. Then, looking around, she saw fresh hoofprints and gigged the Appaloosa forward.

Keeping a close eye on the fresh tracks, she followed their serpentine route through the buttes. It was like a maze she'd once read that a rich man had formed out of hedges. One butte or boulder after another, each a different height and width, each stepping out before her to make her rein the horse either left or right. When she hadn't caught up to the bounty hunter in ten minutes, she grew concerned that she wasn't following his tracks after all.

Her heart pounded and her mouth became dry. Her eyes were large, her brows furrowed. She couldn't imagine being out here alone at this lonely end of the world.

Her voice quivered. "Prophet, goddamnit, where are you?"

"Keep your voice down, will you? You never know who else is out here."

She reined her horse to a quick halt and swung her head right. There he was, in a corridor made by a sandstone scarp and several low, deeply eroded buttes. He stood beside his horse, filling his hat from his canteen.

He was such a welcome sight, she felt like running over and hugging him. Then her anger burned at his leaving her back there.

"What in the hell . . . what in the hell do you think you're doing . . . leaving me back there?"

He shrugged as he held the hat for the horse to drink. "I told you we didn't have time to stop."   .

His nonchalance sent another fire through her. She gripped her saddle horn until her hands turned white, and her voice quivered again, this time with rage. "I have never in my life, Mr. Prophet, met a more arrogant . . . impertinent . . . supercilious cuss than you!"

He regarded her casually as the horse drank from his hat. "I think I know what arrogant means, but the other two words"—he shrugged and shook his head, returning his attention to the horse—"I didn't get much schoolin' back in Georgia, you see. Mostly just picked my daddy's cotton and raided watermelon patches."

"You could have fooled me," she said with taut sarcasm.

"Better get down and give your horse a drink. I'm gonna be pullin' out again in about two minutes."

She was so outraged at his insouciance that her vision swam, and she wanted to scream. Instead, knowing she could very easily be left behind again, she scrambled down from her saddle and, taking his cue, filled her hat from her canteen and fed the water to her horse.

Meanwhile, Prophet donned his wet hat and retrieved his field glasses from his saddlebags. She watched as he climbed a low butte, using rocks and sage clumps for handholds, creating small sand slides in his wake. He gave little indication that his leg was hurting, other than to grunt now and then. He sat near the top of the butte and trained the glasses on the country behind them.

"You see anything?" she called to him.

He didn't say anything as he peered through the glasses. Lowering them, he turned and descended the butte, sliding on his butt over the steepest grades. Limping slightly as he approached his horse, he said, "He's back there, all right. Him and that Big Fifty."

"How do you know?"

He forked leather, took the reins in both hands, and the horse scuttled sideways and back several steps. "Lady, I may not have a whole lot of proper schoolin', but I've been on the owlhoot trail long enough to know when a man with a big gun's doggin' me, and one's doggin' me now. Bank on it."

He spurred his horse into a trot, disappearing around a shelf. She watched him, flabbergasted, and hurried to mount her horse. "Well, wait for me . . . goddamn you, Prophet!"

A mile and a half as the crow flies behind Prophet and Lola Diamond, Dick Dunbar rode his mouse-brown gelding, leaning out from his saddle as he read the sign left by Prophet and the girl's mounts.

Dunbar was a tall, thin man with close-cropped brown hair, a severe, sun-seared face, and a bushy brown mustache drooping around the corners of his grim mouth. On his head was a sweat-soaked bandanna beneath a weather-beaten derby hat he'd swiped from a businessman he'd killed in Alder Gulch two weeks ago. He'd stolen the hat not because he thought it went better with the rest of his attire—faded chambray shirt, rawhide suspenders, dusty broadcloth trousers, and cartridge belt and holster—but because it didn't. He liked the contrast of the hat with the rest of his scruffy clothes and savage-looking weapons, including the big, fifty-caliber rifle perpetually poking out of his saddle sheath.

He thought the hat gave him distinction. It was also a trophy, for the man it had belonged to had been one of Alder Gulch's more prominent businessmen who had, for some reason or another, gotten on the enemies list of

Dick Dunbar's primary employer: Billy Brown.

Billy Brown was why Dunbar was here now. Two days ago he and the other three in his band—the three who'd been so shamefully greased by Lou Prophet and the showgirl—had gotten a cable from Billy's men in Johnson City, telling them to intercept the stage from Henry's Crossing and kill the red-haired showgirl named Lola Diamond and anyone and everyone in her company. The cable hadn't said why. They never did, and Dunbar had learned not to question Billy Brown's motives. But it did say that once the girl was dead, Dunbar and his three associates would be paid one thousand dollars in cash.

One thousand dollars split four ways came to two hundred and fifty dollars, not bad for one girl. One thousand unsplit was even better, and that's why Dunbar felt little but disdain for his fallen comrades, and embarrassment for the way they'd so stupidly walked into Prophet's trap, like calves walking into quicksand. Imagine getting gunned down by a showgirl, which is what had happened to the stupid Sonny Lane!

"Well, I won't tell 'em, Sonny," Dunbar said now as he studied the hoofprints in the tough sod. "I guess that's the least I can do, after you got me on with Billy Brown and all. I'll just say Prophet drygulched all four of us, and I got away . . . somehow."

His face tightened as he considered the "somehow." He decided not to mention the girl opening up with her pea shooter. He certainly wouldn't admit that she'd sent him running for his horse after the last of the other three men were killed and he'd momentarily lost his nerve when the Big Fifty had misfired and the shell had jammed in the breech. He'd say he'd sensed the trap but couldn't convince the others, who rode into it while Dunbar stayed behind, pleading with his brave but foolhardy compatriots to no avail. . . .

Yeah, that should cover Dunbar's ass. Billy Brown couldn't fire him for that. The last thing anyone wanted was to be fired by Billy Brown, because when Billy Brown fired you, he usually killed you in some sneaky, underhanded way when and where you least expected it. Billy Brown didn't like leaving any loose ends, and ex-employees definitely fell into that category.

Satisfied with the story, Dunbar heaved a sigh of relief. Approaching a stretch of open ground, he turned his head to make sure the buffalo gun was still in his saddle boot—the damn thing always misfired when the barrel got hot—then gigged his gelding into a gallop, wanting to eat up some ground between himself and the two he was following. It sure would be nice if he could get this thing over with before nightfall. He'd get himself a good night's sleep, then head back to the main trail to Johnson City first thing in the morning.

It would take him another half day to reach town as it was, packing the girl's body for the reward money, and he couldn't wait to get his hands on that thousand dollars. As long as he'd been killing folks for hire—going on seven years now, and that wasn't counting all the years he'd spent killing Yankee farmers and small-towners with Quantrill's raiders down in Missouri and Arkansas— he'd never once had that much money in his pockets at one time.

Soon the tall, thin gunman with the sunburned face and grim eyes beneath the curled brim of his dusty bowler came to the edge of the badlands. He halted his horse and spat a wad of chew on a flat rock two feet to his left.

"So this is what you had in mind, eh, old boy?" Dunbar said, sending his gaze over the pocked and gouged gray landscape before him.

He'd recognized Prophet when he'd glassed him before he'd tried to ambush him and the girl with the Big Fifty. Prophet had a reputation as a man you didn't mess with, and that was why Dunbar had decided to take the long shot, which had been nudged wide by a sudden wind gust. He rarely missed from that distance, and he sure as hell wouldn't miss again. The damn cannon wouldn't misfire, either, because he'd finish the job with his first two shots.

Also, he'd cut the distance in half. Out there, where he saw a telltale feather of sun-bleached dust lifting about a mile ahead—the dust of two fleeing riders, he was certain—it wouldn't be at all hard to get that close. With all those buttes and rocks for cover, why, a man could practically ride into another man's camp unseen.

Dunbar pulled his bandanna down to his eyes, mopping the sweat from his brows, then shoved it back up on his forehead. Grinning, he gigged his horse into the canyon.

"Damn, Prophet . . . you're makin' this too easy."

17

BLACKFLIES BUZZED.

Cicadas moaned.

The sun beat down on the pale sand and clay, on the dusty yucca leaves, on the sage, and on the rocks strewn here and there about the canyon floor. Lola felt it through her hat. It burned her neck and hands. She had to fold her dress closed to keep it off her exposed leg. She was a fair-skinned girl, and prone to coloring.

There was no water. At least, they hadn't stopped for any fresh, which meant there probably wasn't any. To Lola, it didn't look like a place where there would be much water, except in the rainy seasons—April and September probably. Now the deep, wide gash through which they rode looked like the dry bottom of a long dead lake honeycombed with narrow, winding canyons.

It was an eerie, quiet place, these badlands, with no sign of other people and few of animals. Like several other natural places Lola had visited on the frontier, it had the feeling of having been abandoned by God. Eternity reigned here, the blue sky bowling overhead. It felt like either a sanctified place or an evil one. Lola wasn't sure which.

But she didn't want to die here. She didn't want her bones to become like the ones she saw in the eroded gravel banks, chipped and ground by time, woven into the earth's changing seams, and forgotten.

But then, if she were killed here, whoever killed her would probably take her back to Johnson City for the reward. They'd tie her to the back of a horse, and when they got to town, they'd lift her head by her hair, showing her face to Billy Brown. What would happen to her then? Would they bury her, or take her out in the country and throw her into some canyon?

How odd it felt to be hunted . . . for your body to be worth more dead than alive.

"Watch it—rattlesnake," Prophet warned as Lola, aroused from her reverie, heard the angry hiss.

She looked around and saw a thick diamondback coiled beneath a yucca plant, flicking its tail and tongue, glaring through its coppery eyes, flat as pennies. Her horse contracted its muscles and bucked slightly, veering sideways, then continued down the trail, about thirty feet off the rump of Prophet's mount.

Lola said nothing, just gritted her teeth against her misery—against the heat, her parched throat, sand-gritty eyes, burning shoulder, and aching thighs—and squeezed the reins. Her and Prophet's horses blew and swished their tails at flies as they walked, heads down, shod hooves ringing off stones.

After two hours of steady riding, Prophet stopped to water the horses. While Lola rested in the shade of a gnarled shrub, he limped to the top of a butte shelving over a deep-cut canyon, its walls packed with white bone chips and gravel, and scanned their backtrail through his field glasses.

"He back there?" she asked when he returned.

"Oh, he's back there, all right," Prophet said, replacing the glasses in the case hanging off his saddle.

But from the way he'd said it, she couldn't tell if he'd seen the man with the big rifle, or if he was just relying on his own intuition again, that sixth sense he seemed so proud of. She would have asked him, but his demeanor had become so sour she decided against it. She just got back on her horse, afraid of being left behind, and rode.

They rode so hard that by late afternoon her butt and the backs of her legs were chafed raw and blistering. No matter how she sat, she couldn't get comfortable.

"Prophet . . . please . . . I have to stop," she begged. "I'm not used to this. . . ."

He said nothing, just kept riding straight ahead, swaying with the rhythm of his horse, which he kept to a walk, saving it for a gallop when and if a gallop were needed. Lola was lonely and frightened. Her shoulder ached. She wished Prophet would talk to her, but the big bounty man said nothing. He silently, grimly led the way, kicking up the fine, brown dust behind him.

It was nearly dark when he finally stopped for the day. She'd been dozing in the saddle and was surprised when her own horse came to a halt. She looked around and saw that they were in a hollow surrounded by tall buttes and boulders, a few gnarled shrubs resembling pines. There was a cool breeze which played in Lola's hair and dried the sweat on her face.

Lola tried to dismount but found that her legs and seat were too sore to move. She felt as though her skin had grown into the saddle.

"What are you waiting for?" Prophet asked as he hurriedly stripped the leather off his mount.

"I-I can't move," she said weakly.

She'd never felt this hopeless and weak. Right now she didn't care if the man with the big gun strolled right into their camp, put his big gun up to her head, and pulled the trigger. Here was as good a place to die as anywhere.

Prophet grumbled something as he tossed his saddle in a small alcove that had been carved out of a butte. He approached her, said, "Here," and helped her out of the saddle—none too gently.

"Ouch!"

"Be quiet!" Prophet hissed.

"You opened up my shoulder again . . . and . . . and my butt hurts!" She lowered her head and sobbed like a child.

"Well, crying ain't gonna help. Sit down over there by my saddle and let me get the leather off your horse. I'll tend that shoulder in a minute."

She did as he ordered, not so much sitting as reclining gently on her side, and watched him unsaddle her horse and stake both animals to the gnarled tree only a few feet beyond the camp. He obviously wanted the horses close. Why? In case they had to make a run for it? So they'd warn him if the man with the big gun came calling?

"I cannot get on that horse again tomorrow," she told him as he approached and knelt by her side.

"Let me see that shoulder," he said, gruffly taking her arm.

As he inspected it, holding it out to catch the last light from the fading sky, she studied him soberly. "What in the hell are you so sour about?" she said. "I'm the one getting dragged to my death."

"I ain't sour," he said. "Just busy. Keepin' you alive has become one hell of a job."

"It's not too late to resign."

He started to reply, but she stopped him. "Don't! I don't even want to hear it."

She studied him curiously as he removed a shell from his cartridge belt, then produced a small clasp knife from his jeans. "What are you doing?"

He said nothing as he worked the lead slug from the brass casing with his knife. When he finished, he dropped the slug and said, "Hold your arm out."

"Why?"

"I'm going to cauterize that wound."

"What!"

"It'll stop the bleeding. Hold still and turn your face away."

She wasn't sure what he meant, but it didn't sound good. She drew her arm back and looked at him sharply. "Never mind. It feels much better all of a sudden."

He sighed and regarded her sternly. "Listen, lady, I know what I'm doin'. I'm going to pour this black powder into the wound and light it with a match. That'll cauterize it. If I don't, you're gonna bleed dry by morning."

"Just pack some mud on it."

"We're low on water, and I'll need some to clean my leg."

She stared at his dark visage as she thought it over. Finally, reluctantly, she held out her arm. "This better not hurt."

"Just for a second. Now turn your face away."

She turned her face away and squeezed her eyes closed, wary but finding herself trusting the man. She supposed his type had to do this kind of back-country doctoring all the time.

She heard a match flare and felt a sudden burn on her arm, smelled the acrid odor of gunpowder, burned blood and flesh. As he had promised, the pain lasted only a second. The smell lingered, however, causing her nose to wrinkle.

"Did it work?" she said, inspecting the arm. It stung a little, but not bad. The blood appeared to have clotted.

"Like a charm," he said matter-of-factly, turning to his own wounded leg. "Pull my boot off."

"What?"

"My boot needs to come off," he grouched.

She crawled around in front of him. "What are you so damn grouchy about, anyway?" She grabbed the heel and toe, and gave the boot a solid tug. It slipped halfway off the heel. Another tug, and it came free so quickly she nearly fell over backwards.

Prophet sighed painfully, removed the bandanna from around his calf, and rolled up his blood-soaked jeans. He grabbed the canteen and poured water over the wound, sighing again, whistling through his teeth.

Lola watched him pensively. A thought dawned on her. "Oh . . . I know what it is," she said, brightening.

"Know what what is?" Prophet said, his voice pinched with pain. He took up his clasp knife and opened it.

"What you're so grumpy about."

"I told you I ain't grumpy, just busy. There's a difference. But I wouldn't expect a woman to understand."

"Oh, I understand quite well. You're all bent out of shape because I saved your life."

He paused to look at her dumbly. "What?"

"You're mad because a woman saved your life."

"Oh, for crying out loud!" He removed a box of matches from his shirt pocket, struck a match on his thumbnail, and ran the knife through the flame, sterilizing it. "I never heard anything so stupid in my life."

"That's it! That's it!" she laughed. "You'd rather have died back there than have your hide saved by a woman— a showgirl, to boot!" She laughed once more, for the

moment not feeling her shoulder or the sting of the saddle
in her loins.

She couldn't see his eyes in the dark, but she could
tell from his posture that Prophet was angry. "Listen,
lady, I don't give a shit who saves my hide—if it needs
saving, that is. But my hide didn't need savin'. I was
about to plug that hombre myself. You just beat me to
the punch, that's all. Squeezed off a lucky shot."

She snickered. "Oh, I admit it was a lucky shot, but
the fact that it was fired by a woman—while you were
cowering in the weeds—is going to haunt you till the
day you die. Especially if anyone else gets wind of it.
And believe me, Lou Prophet, if I live to tell the tale,
tell it I certainly will!"

She threw back her head and laughed heartily, tears
rolling down her cheeks. She hadn't felt this good in
days. Suddenly, she was actually enjoying herself. And
at Prophet's expense!

Prophet clasped a hand over her mouth. She stiffened,
giving a startled grunt. Leaning toward her, the bounty
hunter spoke through clenched teeth. "If you don't shut
up, you're gonna lead that hombre with the Big Fifty
right into our camp. Is that what you want?" He shook
her angrily. "Is it?"

Incensed by his impertinence, she would have kicked
him if she'd been standing. As it was, she was defenseless. She glared at him, outraged, her chest rising and
falling heavily. Knowing the only way she could get him
to release her was to shake her head, she did so, her eyes
flashing scorn.

He removed his hand from her mouth.

"How *dare* you!" she rasped from deep in her throat.

He thrust the matches at her. "Now light a match and
hold it next to my leg, so I can see to dig out that slug."

"I certainly will not!"

"If that slug isn't out of my leg pronto, neither one of us will be going anywhere come daylight."

"Is that supposed to be some kind of threat?" she trilled, screwing up her eyes sarcastically. "I've already told you, there's no way I'm getting back on that horse again tomorrow."

"What about the hombre with the Big Fifty . . . and everybody else gunning for you?"

She stiffened, folding her arms stubbornly across her bosom. She started to speak but checked herself. Her body slackened. He was right. If she didn't ride tomorrow, she'd die. And, in spite of how much she ached all over, she really didn't want to die.

"Give me the damn matches," she groused finally, reaching for the box.

She struck a match and held it near his calf, wincing as she saw the blood.

"Hold it close."

"I am."

"Closer."

"You wanna hold your own damn match?"

As he dug the knife point into the jellied wound, she turned away, covering her eyes with her free hand. "Oh, god . . . that's hideous."

"It's not that bad," he said, his voice pinched again with pain. "Ain't that deep. I think I caught a ricochet's all."

"That's all?" she mocked.

"It's not that deep," he repeated absently as he worked, probing the wound with the blade tip, looking for the slug. "And better yet, it didn't hit bone."

"Oh, hush!" she ordered. Inwardly, she was amazed at his courage and resistance to pain. Whatever his faults, he was unlike any many she'd ever known. . . .

The match burned down to her fingers, and she dropped it with an angry "Ouch!"

"Light another one."

"I am, I am. Now where's that stupid box?"

That's how it went for the next several minutes, which seemed like an hour. Prophet dug with the knife while Lola burned her fingers on one match after another.

"Got it!" Prophet said through a quivering sigh, grinding his teeth together. He fished the slug out of the wound and held it up just as the match burned down to Lola's fingers and went out with an angry "Ouch!"

Ten minutes later, Prophet sat back against the butte, his calf once again wrapped with the bandanna. He'd had to spare more water for a mud pack, but it was either that or lose several pints of blood by morning. He was just glad the bullet hadn't gone deeper than it had.

He ate several pieces of the leftover rabbit, which the girl had refused, believing it spoiled. She dozed beside him, her head on her saddle. It was quiet and as dark as velvet. The alcove was capped with stars. Knowing the man with the Big Fifty was close, Prophet hadn't wanted to risk a fire. He could smell the horses, hear them blowing as they slept standing.

He wanted to sleep, as well, knowing he'd need a good rest for tomorrow, but his calf throbbed and he generally felt anxious and out of sorts. He didn't think it was all due to the man stalking them, either.

It was what the girl had said about him being mad because she'd saved his life. He guessed it was true. He'd gotten his tail all twisted and given her the cold shoulder when what he should have done was thank her. If it hadn't been for her good shooting, lucky or not, he'd have been wolf bait.

The thought struck him now like a cold brace from a mountain stream.

He glanced at her lying on her side with her back to him, and shook his head. Wolf bait, sure enough. Imagine that, a pretty little redhead saving his hide with a bullet to a man's forehead. Who would have believed it?

He licked the cigarette paper and twisted it around the tobacco, suppressing a humorous snort. It occurred to him that he might have liked her under different circumstances. He liked how she looked right now, but she was his job, and in his business, you never mixed business with pleasure and lived to tell about it. When he got her to Johnson City, Owen McCreedy would take her into protective custody until the trial, and Prophet would take the money and head back to Henry's Crossing for his horse.

From there, it was on to the next face on the next wanted poster. It wasn't the best life, but it was the best one Prophet had found. Besides, he'd made that pact with the Devil. Behind every face on every wanted poster was one hell of a shindig.

Besides . . . she was awful mouthy.

He smoked the cigarette down, then stubbed it out in the sand. He glanced around one last time, listening closely. Satisfied they were alone, he rested his head on his saddle. He wasn't sure how long he'd slept when he heard a horse whinny.

He sat up quickly and looked at his own two horses, knowing instantly that the whinny had not come from one of them.

There was another horse out there, between fifty and a hundred yards away.

Heart hammering, Prophet climbed slowly to his feet and reached for his gunbelt.

18

PROPHET DECIDED NOT to awaken the girl. She might make noise and give them away, or startle their horses.

He buckled on his gunbelt, grabbed his shotgun, and stole out around the horses as quietly as possible. The faint paling in the east told him it was nearly dawn. He had to be careful; the outlines of objects were growing faintly visible, which meant he would be visible, too.

He crept around a butte, traversed a narrow gully, and hunkered down in a cedar, listening. The morning was still and damp, without a breath of breeze. It was so quiet he thought he could hear the grasshoppers breathing in the thin clumps of bluegrass growing along escarpments and in hollows. A sickle moon angled low in the west. Far away rose the hushed cries of a magpie.

Prophet crouched and cradled the shotgun in his arms. His ears fairly ached with listening. Finally, he heard something. A horse clipping a rock? A man's boot coming down in gravel? Or was it only a stone loosed by gravity down a butte?

Then he heard the unmistakable sound of a horse blowing. He knew it wasn't one of his horses; it had come from farther west, maybe fifty or sixty yards away, behind that big butte yonder.

Prophet hunkered down on his haunches and waited. The trail he and the girl had taken last night passed near here, and if the man with the Big Fifty had risen early to track them, he would pass along their trail.

After about ten minutes, a figure emerged from the gray-black darkness to the west, stealing around the butte. It was a vague figure—only a few lines of a hat, face, and shoulders—but Prophet knew it was the man with the Big Fifty. He breathed gently through his mouth and poked his finger through the eight-gauge's trigger housing.

The man approached slowly, one step at a time. When Prophet could see his outline clearly, a prairie dog chortled about ten feet to Prophet's right. Prophet jumped, startled, heart racing. He cringed, hoping the prairie dog hadn't spooked the tracker. The rodent made a scuttling sound in the weeds as, startled by Prophet, it ran back to its hole.

Gritting his teeth, Prophet returned his gaze westward. The man with the big gun in his arms had stopped, crouching. He stayed that way for over a minute.

"Come on, come on," Prophet silently beseeched the man. "It was nothing. Just a prairie dog. He saw a hawk—that's all. Come on."

The man began walking again, moving slowly this way. He disappeared twice around rocks and shrubs, then appeared again, about thirty feet away. Now Prophet could hear the man's boots grinding gravel; he could hear the anxious rake of his breath in his lungs.

The man approached to within twenty feet of Prophet, bending to study the prints of shod hooves in the powdery dust. He straightened and moved forward, to within twelve feet. Then he was so close that Prophet could have spit on him. He walked on by, slowly following the trail.

When he'd given his entire back to Prophet, he stopped suddenly, like a man startled. He'd either smelled Prophet or felt Prophet's eyes burning a hole through his back. Before the man could react, Prophet stood and thumbed back the shotgun's left hammer. The metallic grating and punctuating click echoed in the heavy silence.

Prophet said quietly, "You know what an eight-gauge loaded with buckshot will do to a man at this range?"

The man froze.

"Let the hammer down on your long gun there and, with one hand, hold it out to me. No, no . . . don't turn this way. Just do what I told you, and make it snappy."

The man cursed through a heavy sigh. There was a slight metallic click as he off-cocked the buffalo gun. Holding it out to Prophet, he said nothing.

Prophet took the gun and, crouching, keeping his eyes on the rifleman, set the rifle on the ground.

"Now, slowly," he said, "unbuckle that gunbelt and let it fall."

"What are you gonna do?" the man asked grimly, the flatness of his voice belying his fear.

"I'm gonna blow a hole through your back big enough to run a train through if you don't drop that gunbelt."

Slowly, with another curse, the man did as he was told, the gunbelt dropping around his boots. Prophet ordered him to kick it away. He said, "You got any more guns on you?"

"That's it."

"Well, I don't believe you. Undress."

"What!"

"Strip down to your skivvies."

"I ain't—!" The man stopped as he turned his head slightly and saw the wide bores of the eight-gauge yawning behind him. He sighed, shook his head, shrugged out of his coat, and started unbuttoning his shirt. Five minutes later, he was standing in the trail, facing Prophet in his undershorts, threadbare wool socks, and bowler hat. Prophet was going through his boots and clothes.

"Yeah, I reckon you were telling the truth," the bounty hunter quipped. "You weren't carryin' any more guns." As he spoke, he withdrew a razor-sharp stiletto from a sheath sewn into the man's right boot. Holding the slender blade up to his face for inspection, he said, "But that there, I bet you wouldn't even feel it goin' in—till it plucked your heart."

The man said nothing.

Prophet tossed the dagger away and stood. "What's your name?"

"Dick Dunbar."

"Dick, I should kill you right now—you realize that, don't you?"

Facing him in his ridiculous garb, the man said nothing. As the sky lightened, the grim expression on his dust-smudged face grew plainer.

"Yeah, you realize that," Prophet said. "But I'll tell you what I'm going to do instead, Dick. I'm going to let you ride back to Billy Brown and tell him I want the bounty on the girl. When I get the bounty, the girl's his."

Still, the man said nothing, but Prophet watched his eyes narrow curiously.

"I'm tired of this shit," Prophet explained. "Tired of busting my ass for a measly hundred and fifty greenbacks. When McCreedy offered me this job, he never told me about you fellas. I don't give a shit whether or not this girl makes it to Johnson City. I'm a bounty hunter, for chrissakes. I take the best I can get, and I have a feelin' I can get a might more than a hundred and fifty dollars from Billy Brown. Tell him I want two thousand five hundred."

Prophet paused, reading the man's grim, befuddled expression.

"Tell him I want two thousand five hundred, and I want it tomorrow at noon in the old mining cabin at the west end of Miner's Gulch. There's an old miner's shack there. When I get the money, he gets the girl. You got that?"

Brows furrowed, the man nodded.

"Tell Billy I want him to deliver the money to me personally. I don't deal with middlemen. If he's afraid of me, he can send his second-in-command. But I want him alone. If I see more than one man, the deal's off. The girl goes free to tell her tale. You got that?"

The man gave a grim nod.

"Good. Now get dressed."

When the man had dressed, Prophet followed him back to his horse and checked the man's saddlebags for more guns, finding an old army-issue forty-four the man was using as a backup, and another knife. Confiscating the weapons, Prophet turned to the man. "Mount up and ride. Remember what I told you, Dick. Two thousand five hundred, and the girl is Billy's."

"You're a son of a bitch," the rider mumbled, forking leather.

"What's that?"

"Nothin'."

"That's what I thought."

When the man had gone, Prophet tossed Dunbar's weapons behind a rock—all but the Big Fifty, that is. The heavy Sharp's in hand, he headed back to the camp.

He stopped suddenly as he approached the horses. The girl stood before him, holding her pocket pistol straight out before her, aimed at Prophet's face.

"You'll never get away with it, you son of a bitch!"

"Hey . . . easy," Prophet said, spreading his hands. "Put that thing down."

"I'll put it down, all right. After I kill you, you lying, cheating, low-down, bounty-hunting bastard!"

"I . . . I take it you overheard," Prophet mused.

"I'll say I overheard. Gonna take the best price you can get, that it, Mr. Prophet?" Her voice was thin and quaking, but tight with outrage. "Two thousand five hundred is a little better than a hundred and fifty. What does it matter if I live or die? At least you'll have your bounty, and that's everything, isn't it?"

"Now just a minute . . ."

She cocked the gun and steadied it. "Just when I was beginning to think you were a man of integrity . . ."

"What you heard me say to that man was a lie. I wanted him to believe I'd exchange you for the bounty so I can get all Brown's men together, and spring a trap on 'em."

"Oh, of course—Billy Brown's gang. You expect me to believe that?"

"Not only Brown's gang, but Billy Brown himself. Owen's gonna have to set him free by noon today if we don't get there. That means he'll be free to supervise the exchange himself, and I have a feeling that, after the thorn you've been in his side, he'll be there. Probably want to drop the hammer on you himself."

Lola watched him, pondering this. "You're lying. Not even you would come up with something that crazy."

He took two steps toward her. "You've been with me long enough to know I'm not the kind of man who'd turn a woman over to Billy Brown. Not for any amount of money . . . not after all the people who've died . . . after all we've been through, the last three days. . . ."

"I heard he has twenty-five men riding for him."

"And I figure about twenty-six will be at Miner's Gulch tomorrow, including Billy himself."

The gun came down several inches. Lola furrowed her eyebrows. "Why . . . ?"

"I have a feeling Owen has more than his hands full with that gang. I know we have. Well, I have a surefire— or, pretty surefire—plan to wipe them out, including Billy."

She dropped the gun to her side. "You're crazy, Prophet."

Prophet nodded and exhaled a ragged sigh. "Maybe so. That's why you're free to go if you want. There's no way I can force you to do what I have in mind for to-morrow. You give me the word, and I'll take you to the stage station over in Skowfield, buy you a ticket for Den-ver. Then I'll go over and help out Owen myself."

"What about the subpoena?"

Prophet shrugged. "It's just a piece of paper. Paper burns right easy, gets lost."

She brushed a strand of hair from her eyes and inclined her head, appraising him, a soft light entering her eyes. "You mean it?"

"Damn tootin'. You've been through enough."

She lifted her dress, resheathing the pistol, and walked away, running her hands through her hair. Two minutes later she turned to him and shook her head. "I don't know, Mr. Prophet, I must be crazy, but I feel inclined to join you to this . . . Miner's Gulch, or whatever you call it."

"You sure?"

"I reckon I've done enough running from Billy Brown.

If I don't play it through, I'll never know if I need to keep looking over my shoulder or not."

Prophet found himself walking toward her. He stopped and gazed into her eyes, lifted to his. "You got sand," he said with a smile.

They stood staring into each other's eyes while the first birds cooed and the horses craned their necks, watching them. Finally, she leaned into him, slowly wrapped an arm around his neck and lifted her head to kiss him. It was a quick kiss, ending when she grew tentative and self-conscious.

He held her, however, and brought her back to him. It was all the encouragement she needed. She brought the other arm up, and held him tightly while they kissed, long and deep, exploring each other's mouths with their tongues. She swiped his hat off, ran a hand through his hair. He released her arms and brought his hands up to her face, caressing her cheeks while he kissed her, liking the swell of her breasts against his chest.

Finally, knowing this was neither the time nor the place, they separated. Their bodies were heavy with want and reluctant to part.

Prophet cleared his throat. "Well," he said, grinning self-consciously. "You . . . kiss right well . . . Miss Diamond."

She smiled and looked down. "You, too . . . Mr. Prophet."

"I reckon we'd better go."

"I reckon."

He reached for her, kissed her once more with the hunger of a man who hadn't kissed a woman in a long time. Then he released her again, and, amazed and befuddled by his feelings, turned to the horses.

"Well, I reckon . . . ," he sighed. "Miner's Gulch . . ."

19

OWEN MCCREEDY SAT in one of the ladder-back chairs by the window and watched the wood-framed clock above his desk. Carved and carefully decorated, the clock had been imported from Switzerland by his great-grandfather. His mother had hauled it from their original home in Massachusetts to Nebraska, and it was the only thing of hers Owen still owned.

It shouldn't hang in this little jailhouse, he mused. It should be in his living room at home, but his wife's family clock hung there, above the mantel. Owen had once thought his mother's clock lent his shabby little office a touch of sophistication. He saw now, however, that teakwood and brass and hand-tooled detailing looked about as appropriate in this room, with its rusty stove, battered rolltop, mud-brick walls, and grungy puncheon floor, as would a tea set of Bavarian china. It served only to make the place look even more dour in contrast.

Why he was thinking this at the moment, however, McCreedy couldn't explain. Maybe because he didn't want to think of the time the clock registered—two minutes to noon. Two minutes till the time he was under orders from the judge to release Billy Brown if the girl had not shown, which she hadn't. No, she and Prophet had not shown, and in two minutes, Owen McCreedy would have to produce his keys from his desk drawer and open Billy Brown's cell, endure the grins and taunts and muttered threats and watch the little Irish bastard saunter out of the dingy little jailhouse with its out-of-place Swiss clock, free as the breeze.

McCreedy sipped his coffee and watched the minute hand click another minute closer to noon. It dawned on him now why the clock no longer looked appropriate in here. Once, it had represented all his hopes and dreams for the office of sheriff. Now it symbolized only failure— the naïveté of those dreams in a town dominated by a bottom-feeding scoundrel like Billy Brown.

Billy had won. Prophet and the girl probably lay dead in a ravine somewhere.

And that damn clock was coming down. . . .

McCreedy had started to rise when his office door opened. "Knock-knock," sang Hart Baldridge, who entered with his customary flare, clasping a fresh shirt for his client and the new edition of the *Johnson City Chronicle* in his beringed right hand. The county judge, Norman Howe, entered behind him—a compact man with a red face and turkey neck. The judge politely removed his slouch hat and held it in both hands.

McCreedy sat back down in his chair and heaved a heavy sigh. Baldridge inhaled deeply, but before he could speak, McCreedy said, "Yeah, yeah, it's high noon. You know where the keys are, Baldy."

"Uh . . . that's Bald*ridge*," the attorney corrected, heading for the desk.

When he'd gone back into the cell block, Judge Howe shoved his hands in the pockets of his brown suit pants and gave McCreedy a sympathetic scowl. "Sorry, Owen," he said. "I wish I could've given you more time, but the law says—"

"I know you do, Judge," McCreedy said. "Truth of it is, though, it wouldn't have mattered if you'd have given me *three* weeks to get the girl here. She and Prophet are dead. I don't have, and never would have had, a witness. It's my own damn fault."

"We could still call a trial . . . call Perry to testify . . ."

McCreedy shook his head. "We'd never get a conviction on circumstantial evidence, Judge. You know that as well as I do. And I'm not willing to lessen the charge. I want him to hang . . . and I want all the trash he has working for him out of here. That's the only way this town will ever civilize, become the place you and me and the rest of the law-abiding citizens want it to be."

"Well . . . maybe next time," Judge Howe said, turning to gaze troubledly at the cell block door.

Once more McCreedy shook his head. "There ain't gonna be any next time for me, Judge. I'm throwing in the badge. I'm gonna go get Alice, and we're gonna get the hell out of here."

The judge turned his scowling eyes back on McCreedy. "Owen, you're a good man. You'll get Brown, sooner or later. You can't leave this town. I won't let you. You're the first good sheriff we've had here. Why, without you . . ."

"Without me, you might've gotten rid of Billy and his gang by now."

"You're selling yourself only half a load there, Owen.

This is a tough town . . . always has been. You need to give yourself more time—"

The door to the cell block opened, and Billy Brown strolled in with his chest puffed out. He was grinning like a circus clown as he walked up to McCreedy, a cigarette wedged in the left corner of his mouth. His curly gray hair was combed back damp, and he wore a wrinkled vest over his fresh silk shirt. The newspaper Baldridge had brought him was folded under an arm. He held out his hand for McCreedy to shake.

"Well, it was a nice try, anyway, McCreedy. I'll give you that." He was fairly exploding with contained laughter.

McCreedy did not shake the criminal's hand. He just gazed grimly, hatefully into Billy Brown's cunning eyes.

Billy shrugged. "No? Well, okay, then. See ya around, McCreedy."

He glanced at Baldridge, who stood behind him on his boot heels, proudly fingering his suspenders, and the two men headed for the door and outside. Apparently, several of Billy's men were waiting by the hitchrack: Loud whoops rose as Billy and the attorney walked out the office door.

McCreedy sat in his ladder-back chair, staring at the clock. Judge Howe stood before him and to one side, fists in his pockets, head bowed as if in prayer. When the whoops and congratulations faded outside, and Billy Brown and his entourage had wandered off to a saloon, Howe cleared his throat and regarded McCreedy soberly.

"Well, I hope you change your mind, Owen. I surely do. There's always another battle . . . especially with a man like Brown."

With that he turned slowly and walked to the door. Once there, he turned back to McCreedy and opened his mouth to speak. He stopped, shook his head, and continued outside, closing the door softly behind him.

McCreedy pushed himself out of his chair and set his empty coffee cup on his desk. He looked at the clock, pondering it for several seconds. Finally, he removed his badge from his vest, tossed it into a drawer, and reached up with both hands to remove the clock from the wall.

With the clock under his left arm, he left the office and headed west up Main Street, which was choked with carts and wagons loaded with dry goods and mining equipment. The boom was on—had been for a good two years now, which made the pickings ripe for a man like Billy Brown.

McCreedy had walked two blocks toward his house when commotion on the street behind him made him stop and turn around. About a block away, a man on horseback was yelling at a buckboard driver to get out of his way. When the buckboard had moved out from the loading dock before Metzenbaum's Mercantile, the rider gigged his horse into a gallop past McCreedy.

Horse and rider, both sweat-lathered and out of breath, looked as though they'd come a long way at a killing pace. At first, McCreedy thought the man was a ranch hand fetching a doctor. But the man did not ride up to Doc Kyle's place on the corner of First Avenue. He stopped instead before the Nuremberg, the most expensive hotel in town. Climbing swiftly out of his saddle, he gave his reins a few cursory loops over the hitchrack, took the porch steps two at a time, and ran through the hotel's double glass doors, nearly busting the glass out of one in the process.

McCreedy stood scowling suspiciously at the Nuremberg's brick facade. It was in the Nuremberg that Billy Brown had his headquarters, in a posh, pile-carpeted office on the third floor. McCreedy often saw the crime boss standing out on his balcony, smoking cigarettes as he gazed down at "his" town, like some thick-necked, round-bellied lord, his pudgy hands on the wrought-iron railing, a self-satisfied cast to his arrogant gaze.

The rider had to be one of Billy's men. If so, where had he come from in such a hurry, bearing what urgent news for Billy?

After about a minute and a quarter, the man reappeared through the double doors, turned left, and ran east down the boardwalk, tracing a circuitous route through the throng of shoppers and businessmen. When he'd run a block, he turned into Billy Brown's favorite saloon—where Billy was no doubt celebrating his release from the hoosegow.

McCreedy stood there staring eastward down the street for several seconds, his brows furrowed with contemplation. Finally, he walked over to Miller's Livery Barn, and got Miller's son Fred to take a ride into the mountains looking for Perry Moon.

"Tell him I need him here pronto," McCreedy told the raw-boned kid with a wavy thatch of bone-white hair. When he gave the kid directions to his deputy's hunting shack, the kid said, "What's the matter, Sheriff? Trouble?"

"Maybe," McCreedy said, thoughtfully prodding a molar with his tongue. "Maybe not."

He left the kid saddling a stout gelding, and headed back to the jailhouse with his clock.

"Mr. Brown! Mr. Brown!"

Billy had just tossed back a shot of Spanish brandy and was about to chase it with beer when he heard the refrain, and saw the man run toward him from the door, weaving between tables. The voice was so loud that everyone at Billy's table—Baldridge, Billy's *segundo,* Clive Russo, and several others including a few card

dealers and pleasure girls Billy kept on retainers—turned
to watch the man approach.

It was Dick Dunbar, looking wrung out and peaked,
his bowler ready to fall off his head. Hadn't he been sent
out after Prophet and the girl?

Dunbar stopped and grabbed Baldridge's chairback for
support, staring across the table at Billy. "Mr. Brown . . .
we got trouble." He was huffing and puffing like an old
woman, and his unshaven face was drawn, eyes wild. It
was a distasteful display. Billy didn't like to see his men
lose their composure like this, no matter what kind of
trouble they'd gotten themselves into.

Grimacing like he'd swallowed camphor, Billy turned
to Clive Russo and jerked his head to indicate one of the
private rooms on the second floor. Scraping his chair
back, Billy grabbed his half-smoked cigarette from the
ash tray, and headed for the stairs at the back of the
saloon. Dick Dunbar and Clive Russo followed Billy up
the stairs and into one of the gambling rooms.

Billy dropped into an arm chair at the baize-covered
poker table, holding his cigarette over an ash tray, and
waited for Clive Russo to close the door. Dick Dunbar
stood facing Billy demurely. Sweat and dust streaked his
face. Suddenly remembering, he removed his hat from
his head, and held it awkwardly before him.

"Okay, what's this about?" Billy snapped when Russo
had closed the door.

"I found the girl and Prophet," Dunbar said. "But"—
he sighed and shook his head, unable to meet Billy's
searing gaze—"you ain't gonna like it."

"Where's your gunbelt?" Billy asked him, exhaling
smoke through his nostrils. Immediately, he knew it was
the wrong question to ask. It threw the man off. Obviously, he'd been relieved of the damn thing. "Forget it—
what about the girl?"

Dunbar swallowed. He was thinking he should've just taken off after he'd run into Prophet, headed to Texas or California. Never should've gone back to Billy after he'd been bested by Prophet. It was just that the money was so damn good. . . .

He licked his lips. "Well, me and Ralph and Donna, we was trailin' Prophet back in the—"

"Skip ahead, skip ahead," Billy snarled with an impatient wave of his hand.

"Well . . . I was the only one who made it out of there alive, on account of I'm right handy with my long gun, an—"

"Skip *ahead*!" Billy roared. "I have a beer, a bottle of Spanish brandy, and a plump whore waiting for me *downstairs*!"

Visibly shaken, Dunbar shook his head as if to clear the cobwebs. He stared at the table, the midday light reflected off the baize. "Prophet . . . said he'll turn the girl over to you . . . for two thousand five hundred."

Billy sneered, anger mottling his face. "He did, did he?"

"That's what he said, sir."

"Where is this exchange supposed to take place?"

"The old miner's cabin in Miner's Gulch tomorrow at noon. He said no sooner and no later."

Billy raised his eyebrows, indignant. "Oh, he did, did he?" He looked at Russo.

Clive shrugged. "Thinks he can get more from you than he was getting from McCreedy."

"Yeah, well . . . he's a bounty hunter," Billy muttered distastefully. He sucked on his cigarette, narrowing his eyes thoughtfully. "Miner's Gulch, eh?" he asked Dunbar.

"That's right, sir. Miner's Gulch."

"Noon tomorrow."

"Yes, sir."

Billy was nodding.

"What do you want to do, Billy?" Clive asked through his Custer-style mustache. "Could be Prophet and the sheriff are in cahoots. Could be a trap."

Billy shook his head. "Nah. I just left the sheriff. He's ready to quit. And even if Prophet's got somethin' up his sleeve, he's only one man, with a girl."

Billy sat back in his chair, smoking his cigarette and staring at the wall above the door, his tiny eyes darting this way and that.

"We meet him," he said with an air of finality, through the smoke hovering about his head. "And just in case it is a trap, we meet him with all the men we have—armed with Winchesters. Can you gather them all by tomorrow?"

"No problem, Billy."

Billy got up and stubbed out his cigarette in the ash tray. Sidling up to Dunbar, he threw a brotherly arm over the man's shoulders, and grinned in his sweat-beaded face. "Dick, tell me . . . how'd he get your gun?"

Dunbar shifted uncomfortably, glanced at Billy, then at Clive, the corners of his mouth twitching a grin. "Well . . . I was creeping into his camp this mornin', you see, an' . . . an' somehow the son of a bitch winded me, an—"

Billy patted the man's shoulder, cutting him off. "That's okay, Dick. 'Nough said."

He turned and grabbed the doorknob. On his way out, he glanced at Clive, then at Dunbar, and made a slashing motion across his throat.

20

"WHO ARE YOU, anyway, Prophet?"

It was high noon, and they'd been riding leisurely for most of the morning, climbing gradually out of the badlands and into foothills, the air gradually cooling, drying the sweat on horses and riders. Pines and firs loomed around them on mountain slopes, and here and there they came upon ravines, deep with buffalo grass and dotted with lichen-flecked granite boulders. Prophet kept his eyes skinned for bears, as this was grizzly country.

Lola's question had come out of nowhere, surprising him. Since their brief passion earlier, they'd been shy around each other, and hadn't said much.

He glanced back at her for several seconds, then returned his eyes to the game trail they were following south. "Me . . . I'm a Georgia farmboy," he said, accentuating his accent. "Ah come west to make a name for m'self, I did." He chuffed a laugh. "Quite the name I've made."

"You fight in the war?"

"I was with Hood at Utoy Creek and with Longstreet at Ringgold Gap—practically fighting in my own backyard. Lost a cousin and a good many friends in both battles. Pickett's Mill and Lovejoy's Station took two more cousins and an uncle."

There was a silence punctuated by the sounds of their horses breathing against their bits, squeaking saddle leather, and hooves clacking along the rocky trail. It was awkward for her to be suddenly liking this man.

"What brought you to bounty hunting?" she asked.

"Fell into it when a buddy of mine was killed in Abilene, Kansas. I'd been drinking for about three days straight, and finally went back to the cow camp. Well, ole Clay never made it back. Turned out a couple of Mexicans killed him in an alley and took his gambling winnings. I'd seen them earlier, sort of knew who they were, and I tracked 'em down in Texas, along the Brazos, and killed 'em both."

He glanced at the girl to gauge her reaction, but she was staring blandly at the bobbing head of her horse.

He continued, "Well, I brought them both back to Abilene and found out they each had a bounty on them—five hundred dollars. I collected the bounty, decided that two days work for a thousand dollars was a hell of a lot easier than riding herd for thirty a month and found, and . . . well"—he smiled halfheartedly—"here I am."

"Yes," she said dryly. "And here I am."

"Sorry about that."

"No, you're not, and you know what?"

"What's that?"

"Neither am I . . . any longer."

Staring straight ahead, he smiled.

"What do you do with your money?" she asked.

"Have fun."

"What's that?" she called behind him.

He stopped his horse and swung around to face her.

"After the war, I made a deal with the Devil. I told ole Scratch if he let me have enough fun to forget all my armless and legless friends and family and that awful death-stink, why, I'd shovel all the coal he wanted down in Hell."

"The Devil and Lou Prophet on the same side—Lord help us all."

Prophet laughed.

"That's me—what about you?" he asked after they'd started moving again.

She told him about her years learning acting from East Coast thespians, about her journey west and the unfulfilled dreams of playing in the big houses in San Francisco and Denver. About playing vaudeville and Shakespeare in backstreet taverns where the cowboys and miners and every jasper in between drank and gambled and howled, eyeing her lewdly and mouthing obscenities.

"We might as well have been reciting the alphabet as Shakespeare, for all the appreciation we got," she griped. "But you know what?"

"What's that?" he said over his shoulder.

"I'm going to make it big someday, Lou."

"Lola, I wouldn't put it past you."

Two hours later they came to a picturesque creek flowing through a narrow valley, heavily forested on one side, grassy on the other. The black water slid almost soundlessly in its deep bed, on the banks of which Indian paintbrush and balsamroot grew thickly.

Prophet halted his horse where the bank dipped low to the water and there was a brief, sandy shore and a fallen aspen, the break charred from a lightning strike. Squirrels and mountain chickadees chattered in the branches.

"What a heavenly place," Lola said. "Are we stopping here?"

"Why not?" Prophet said, heavily dismounting. "I don't know about you, but my butt feels like I been straddling an anvil for seven days straight."

"Oh, god!" Lola cried, concurring. Wincing against the pain, she climbed out of the leather. "How far do we have left?"

"Oh, about two miles."

She looked at him with wide-eyed surprise. "Really?"

He pointed above the grassy hill on the other side of the creek. "See those two peaks up yonder—the pointy one and the one that looks like . . . uh . . . ?"

"A breast?" she finished for him, narrowing her eyes and giving him a schoolmarm's tolerant smile.

"Yeah, that's the one. Well, Miner's Gulch's just on the other side of those."

"Isn't it dangerous, being this close? What if Billy sends out riders to scour the area for us?"

"He'll be expecting us on the north side of the canyon, over there. We're on the south side. We made a wide circle around Johnson City, which is right over there, about seven miles as the crow flies."

She smiled at him admiringly. "You are truly a man of the country, aren't you, Mr. Prophet?"

He smiled back. "I'll take that as a compliment, Miss Diamond."

"As it was meant, Mr. Prophet."

With a sigh, he turned to unsaddle his horse. When he had the leather off both mounts, he led them down to the creek for water, then picketed them on the other side, where the grass grew so thick it slumped under its own weight.

She sat on the opposite bank, feet drawn up, watching

him, liking the tall, gangly ruggedness of the man, liking the way his shoulders pulled his sweaty shirt taut across his back, liking the way he talked gently to the horses as he carefully rubbed them down with handfuls of grass. She'd never expected to fancy such a man, having favored only those men of the city she'd considered cultured. She doubted Lou Prophet had ever read a book in his life—beyond a few Bible verses as a boy.

She removed her straw hat and shook out her hair. What would her mother think? She wasn't sure what she thought herself—only that she had found herself feeling very close to this man who had nearly gotten her killed. But if it hadn't been for him, she'd still be running from Billy Brown, feeling like a rabbit stalked by a pack of angry wolves. As it was now—hell, she was gunning for Billy Brown!

Prophet waded back across the creek, the water rising to his waist. "I'm gonna go see what I can find for supper," he said as he climbed the bank, heading for his shotgun. "You still have your pea-shooter, don't you?"

"Don't worry about me," she said, patting her thigh.

He shook his head and walked west along the creek, then followed a twisting game trail up the mountain on his left, ducking under branches, the needle-carpeted turf crunching softly beneath his boots. Topping the mountain, he discovered a brushy cut in the valley on the other side. Descending the cut, he flushed a covey of grouse and brought down three with both barrels of the eight-gauge.

The buckshot tore one of the birds nearly in two. One was little better off, but the third bird was only winged. He chased it down, wrung its neck, and, the three birds in tow, headed back up the mountain, then down through the woods toward the creek.

Approaching their encampment, he stopped suddenly when he saw Lola's green dress, chemise, bloomers, and pistol sheath lying in the grass near the creek. Then he heard a splash and Lola's voice, gently chiding: "You're back awfully soon."

His eyes found her in the water, about thirty yards up the creek, where the bank spread briefly and the cool, black water deepened in a gently swirling pool. He spread a toothy grin.

"A gentleman would avert his eyes," she said.

"I ain't no gentleman."

"Turn away—I'm bathing."

"I'll join you," Prophet said, sitting down to remove his boots.

"No!"

Her protests fell on deaf ears. In a minute, Prophet had set the birds on the aspen and peeled out of his grimy clothes, tossing away his ragged underwear, and, naked as the day he was born, strode off the bank and into the water, lifting his arms and wincing against the cold.

"Good Lord—this must be snowmelt!" he shrieked.

"You just stay down there," she ordered, petulant, only her head and neck above the water. "This is my pool."

"Ah, that feels good!" he cooed, diving in and coming up, shaking his head like a wet dog. "Ohhh, *Lordy,* I needed that!"

He put his head down and splashed toward her. When the sandy bottom dropped away into the pool, Prophet dove deep, opening his eyes and watching her lovely, delicate body grow toward him, her arms covering her breasts. She turned and tried to swim away, but he grabbed her foot and pulled her back.

Resurfacing, he heard her admonishing protests: "Lou Prophet, a lady is *bathing*!"

"She sure the hell is!" he laughed, trying to embrace her.

She shrieked and kicked away from him, splashing, but it was only a halfhearted attempt, and in a moment she was in his arms, relaxing in his embrace, letting his lips find hers, throwing her arms around his shoulders. When he drew his lips away, she brushed water from her eyes, a coy smile working at her lovely mouth.

"Mr. Prophet, you are an ill-mannered man."

"A reprobate."

"An unguarded lady is unsafe in your company."

He was nuzzling her neck, biting her ear. She giggled. He said, "Don't worry. This cold water's about rendered me harmless."

She couldn't help imagining her mother's disapproval—her cultivated daughter frolicking in a mountain stream with a frontier bounty hunter! It passed quickly, however, and was replaced by an enormous sense of freedom and happiness, a transcendent appreciation for this big, muscular man in her arms. How far she'd come from the frightened, angry, miserable young woman she'd been less than twenty-four hours ago. . . .

Sorry, Mother . . .

She reached for Prophet's member. "Oh, my! The cold does have a rather . . . stifling effect."

"Yep, I don't think . . ." He stopped as she stroked him.

"Getting better?"

He didn't say anything. Finally, wordlessly, he pulled her to the bank, watching her breasts rise above the water, the water dripping over them in small cascades, streaming down her belly. He backed her against the sandy bank, only her upper body out of the water. She sat in the sand, the water washing over her legs. He held

her arms gently above her head as he kissed her and
gently spread her knees, working his hard belly between
them. . . .

"I'm afraid, Lou," she said.

"Don't be afraid."

"What if I've fallen in love with you?"

He looked at her. "If you have, you won't be for long.
That's just the way it's always been with me."

She gazed deeply into his eyes.

"Tell me to quit and I'll quit," he said.

She placed her hands on both sides of his head, and
covered his mouth with hers, drawing her knees up to
his sides. . . .

They made love for most of the rest of the afternoon.

When the sun had sunk behind the mountains, filling
the valley with a cool, early night, Prophet built a fire,
roasted the birds, and boiled coffee. They talked lazily
as they ate, and when they'd finished eating, they made
love again by the fire.

They lay in each other's arms, the fire snapping and
hissing beside them, shunting shadows against the forest,
and he quelled her fears about tomorrow, telling her exactly how it would be and what she would do, but re-
minding her over and over that she had only to give him
the word and they'd head to the stage station at Skowfield.

Finally, she drifted off to sleep, and Prophet lay there,
liking the feel of her curled up next to him, her head on
his arm, staring up at the soft night sky, the clouds drift-
ing like smoke under the stars. It would've been a perfect
night without the anxiety about tomorrow, his reluctance
at using as bait for Billy Brown this woman he'd just
made love to.

Feeling an urge for a cigarette, he gently slipped his arm out from beneath her and rose, covering her again with the blanket. He dressed in his jeans, boots, and socks, and threw a blanket over his shoulders, then retrieved his makings sack from his shirt. Taking a seat on the aspen, he plucked a paper from the canvas sack and drew a line across it with tobacco.

As he rolled and lit the cigarette and then sat smoking it, staring across the moving water reflecting the umber glow of the dying fire, he thought about tomorrow.

If Billy Brown had twenty-five men riding for him, Prophet was sure all or nearly all would be at Miner's Gulch tomorrow at noon. Twenty-six men, including Billy himself, against one broken-down bounty hunter and a showgirl.

Prophet had to smile at that. He shook his head. He had to be nuts. All he really had on his side was his knowledge of the canyon, for he'd helped out a mining buddy there several years ago, when some silver and a smattering of gold remained, before the silver prices fell and the frequent rock slides made it too dangerous for even the most die-hard of pick-and-shovelers. Mining wasn't his style—never had been. He liked the saddle too much, the feel of a horse beneath him, and he liked moving around too much, which was funny, since the Prophet clan had lived in the north Georgia mountains for generations.

He'd had to go and turn out the black sheep of the family. . . . Or was it the war that had made him restless, the memories making him run . . . ?

When he finished the cigarette, he poured a cup of coffee and cleaned his guns, finishing up with the Big Fifty he'd taken from Dick Dunbar. Tomorrow, he'd need all the help he could get.

He finished his coffee, drank water from the stream, and bedded down, hoping against hope that the trap he intended for Billy Brown wouldn't snare him and Lola, as well. . . .

21

OWEN MCCREEDY WAS stretched out in one of the jail cells when he heard the front door open and Perry Moon's voice. "Boss?"

McCreedy sat up slowly, dropping his feet to the floor. Rubbing the sleep from his eyes—when was the last time he'd slept for more than two hours at a time?—he said, "Yeah, back here. I'm comin'."

Yawning, he stood, rubbed his bristly face, patted his sandy hair down, and walked heavily out the cell door, down the short hall, and into his office. Perry Moon's saddlebags and rifle were lying just inside the door, but Moon himself was nowhere to be seen. McCreedy frowned curiously. Then Perry himself appeared in the door, carrying the packs and panniers he'd taken off his pack horse and in which he'd carried two weeks' worth of provisions. The packs looked plenty light now, however.

When he saw McCreedy, the young deputy stopped suddenly, boyishly wide-eyed. "Did ye get him, Boss?"

McCreedy shook his head. "Not yet."

"Oh, dang it all, anyway!" the tall twenty-two-year-old complained, his face twisted with dismay. McCreedy had always thought Perry's name fit him, for his face was moon-shaped, though now it was covered with a thin beard, and the knobs of his cheeks and nose were peeling from sunburn. His clothes were filthy, and McCreedy could smell the lad from here.

As he came through the door and set the pannier next to his saddlebags, McCreedy said, "I bet you were running low on supplies."

"Oh, I still had some coffee and flour left, and a little sugar. It wasn't no problem, Boss. Pa always said a man could survive his whole life on just flour and coffee from town. The rest he could find out in the wild."

"Yeah, and your old man nearly did just that, didn't he?" McCreedy said, remembering Perry's father, Jake Moon, one of the original settlers of Johnson City who'd been lured to the region by silver and gold. Eight years ago, he'd died in a rockslide in Silver Canyon.

"He sure did."

"Well . . . I'm sorry I had to put you through that, Perry. Two weeks alone in those mountains is a long time, but I thought it was better than you having some so-called 'accident' here in town. Your ma never would've forgiven me for that."

Perry was kneeling down, pulling articles out of the saddlebags. "Well, I ain't afraid of Billy Brown, but I see why you wanted me to lay low for a while." He stood with several boxes of forty-four cartridges and placed them in the bottom drawer of McCreedy's desk. Closing the drawer, he turned to the sheriff with a brooding look on his face. "So what are we gonna do about Billy, Boss?"

A dark cast shading his features, McCreedy went to the stove and poured himself a cup of coffee. "Well, that's why I had Fred fetch you, Perry. The girl didn't show, so's there hasn't been a hearing or trial. But something happened earlier that makes me believe she and Prophet might still be alive. A rider stormed into town earlier—one of Billy's riders. He had urgent news for Billy, and something tells me that news has something to do with Prophet and the girl. The man looked like someone had hornswoggled him good. He wasn't happy at all." Thoughtfully, McCreedy blew on his coffee and sipped.

The deputy was locking his rifle in the gun rack. "You think they got Proph on the run?"

"Either that or holed up somewhere. Maybe in a line shack or an old trapper's cabin, and they're havin' a hard time rootin' 'im out." McCreedy shook his head. "I don't know . . . it's hard to figure. If that's the case, why didn't Billy and his men ride out immediately?"

"Maybe he figured it'd look too suspicious—him ridin' out with a pack like that, right after that hombre stormed in here so fast. Maybe he figured you was watchin'."

Pursing his lips and nodding, the sheriff said, "That could be." The only problem with young Moon's scenario was that McCreedy didn't think Billy Brown respected him enough to worry whether or not he was watching.

"I don't know," McCreedy said disgustedly, after a long silence. "Maybe it doesn't have anything to do with Prophet and the girl. But I brought you back to hold down the fort. If Billy and his men leave town, I'm going to trail 'em, see where they head. So why don't you run over to the Excelsior and get yourself a big steak and plate of beans, then go on home for a bath and some shut-eye. Come back here first thing in the morning."

"Sounds good to me, Boss," Perry Moon said with a tired sigh, picking up his saddlebags and heading for the door.

"Oh, Perry," McCreedy called. He tossed the lad a coin. "Here's for that meal. Tell 'em you want the best in the house."

"Thanks, Boss," the lad said, glancing at the coin and smiling.

"See you tomorrow."

"First thing."

As the deputy led his horses toward the feed barn, McCreedy stepped outside and cast his gaze up the lamp-lit street to the Nuremberg, where all the windows were lit, a half-dozen horses nosed the hitchrail, and the sounds of the roulette wheel clattered in the cool mountain air.

He turned, pulled a chair outside, and sat under the portico, watching the Nuremberg for signs of anything suspicious—namely Billy Brown heading out with his riders. McCreedy didn't think he'd leave at this time of night if he hadn't left earlier, but he wasn't taking any chances. When he did leave—if he left—McCreedy wanted to know about it, so he could dog him.

At one A.M., McCreedy decided nothing was going to happen. Needing at least a few hours' rest if he was going to be at all effective tomorrow, he retired to the cell in which he'd been sleeping earlier, and lay down with a weary groan.

When would it end? When would he finally have Billy Brown behind bars? When could he finally retrieve his wife from the Holbrook farm, where he'd sequestered her after arresting Billy? When could he and Alice start living their lives again?

Fortunately, he was so tired that the questions didn't haunt him long. Before he knew it, sunlight streamed through the barred window above his head, and he heard boots clomping on the wood floor, getting louder as they approached. "Boss?"

It was Perry Moon.

"Oh, shit!" McCreedy griped, swinging his feet to the floor. "How long did I sleep?"

"Well . . . it's pret' near nine o'clock."

McCreedy was pulling his boots on. "You see any movement around the Nuremberg, Perry?"

"That's why I came in to wake ye. Billy Brown and Clive Russo just had a couple horses brought up from the feed barn. Fred Miller came and told me."

"Fred?"

"Yeah, when I delivered my horses last night, I told him to let us know if Billy called for his saddle horse."

"Goddamn—that's good thinkin', son," McCreedy said, putting a hand on his deputy's shoulder. The young man had been McCreedy's deputy for only three months—the last had been scared off by Billy Brown—but he was catching on quick. "Thanks."

"Before I come to wake ye, they were still tied to the hitchrack," the proud deputy called to his boss, as McCreedy stomped down the hall and into his office.

He made a beeline for the window and looked out at an angle, up toward the hotel swathed in morning sunshine. Billy Brown and Clive Russo had just stepped through the Nuremberg's double doors, pulling their gloves on and adjusting their hats—the squat, thick-set Billy and the six-foot, slender Russo with his ostentatious red mustache and goatee, which, it was said, a Chinese courtesan washed and combed every morning in his room across from Billy's in the Nuremberg.

"Yeah, here they come," McCreedy breathed.

He grabbed his gunbelt from the peg by the door and strapped it around his waist, then walked to the gun rack for a thirty-thirty. He grabbed a box of shells from a desk drawer. Having seen Perry's horse at the hitchrack, he said, "I'll take your horse. I'll see you in a couple hours . . . I hope."

"If ye don't?" Perry called as McCreedy headed out.

McCreedy thought about this. "If I don't, you just got a promotion."

The sheriff stepped outside and cast his gaze to his left, where Brown and Russo were cantering their horses eastward, away from McCreedy. They turned right and disappeared behind a blacksmith shop, the chimney of which filled the bright air with sooty black smoke. McCreedy shoved his rifle into Perry's saddle boot, mounted up, and gigged the horse past the Nuremberg, tracing Brown's course around the blacksmith shop and down First Street, which curved around a mountain. Along the mountain's base, falling-down shanties belched breakfast smoke, and a three-legged cur barked at McCreedy's horse trotting past.

"Go lay down, Lucky," the sheriff growled, checking the horse's frightened sidestep.

First Street played out down a steep grade. At the bottom of the grade and about a half-mile from Main Street sat the rodeo grounds, in a wide, flat bend in the river. Just before McCreedy came to the road forking off to the grounds, he dismounted his horse and tethered it to a cottonwood along a rocky butte. Stealing along the butte, he removed his hat, and, keeping the butte between him and the rodeo grounds, stole a look toward the river.

Near the rough wooden spectator bleachers, Billy Brown and Clive Russo were cantering their horses toward a loose pack of riders—over twenty by McCreedy's estimation. All were armed with pistols, rifles, and knives, extra cartridge belts looped across their chests. They watched their approaching boss and his *segundo*— ready to ride, the kill-lust plain in their eyes.

McCreedy's heart rattled a harried rhythm as he watched Brown and Russo bring their horses to a halt before the army. Billy's head jerked as he issued orders. Then he gigged his horse through the crowd, Clive following, and headed across the rodeo grounds toward the tree-lined river reflecting the morning sunshine. The grim warriors reined their horses in 360-degree circles, and galloped up to their leader as Brown and Russo reached the river.

McCreedy whistled softly as he watched the group splash through the river and mount the butte on the other side. What he could do against twenty-five men, he had no idea, but it was too late to swear in more deputies. If he did nothing else, he could see where they were headed and what they were up to. If they had Prophet cornered, he owed the man a hand, however feeble.

He waited until they'd all disappeared down the other side of the butte and were gone, only their chalky dust lingering in the cottonwoods. Then he turned, untied his horse from the cottonwood, and mounted up, galloping toward the stream.

Brown and his men were deep in the mountains when Billy called a halt to rest the horses, as they were showing signs of altitude fatigue.

"Billy, you think we should leave a couple men behind to watch our backtrail?" Clive Russo asked as his boss stood holding his horse's reins while puffing a cigarette down to his fingers.

"You thinking McCreedy might've followed us?" Brown said with a caustic snort.

Russo shrugged. He'd removed his hat, and his thin

red hair hung wetly to his shoulders. "Never know. Why take a chance?"

"Well, I ain't afraid of Owen McCreedy, but if it'll make you feel better, Clive . . ."

Russo turned to where the men milled along the trail ambling through the pine forest. Gentle, shaded slopes lifted on both sides. Birds and squirrels chittered. The ground was dappled with sunlight and gave off the smell of moist earth and pine needles.

"Beach, Gruber," Clive said. "Hang back in case we're bein' dogged."

"And if we are . . . ?" Gruber asked.

Clive turned to Billy, a question in his eyes.

"Shoot 'em," Billy said, as though imparting obvious information to a simpleton. Then he flicked away his cigarette stub. Bouncing on his right foot, he hiked his left boot into his stirrup and grunted into the leather. "The rest of you, let's ride!"

While the others rode away, disappearing around a bend in the wooded trail, Beach and Gruber glanced at each other meaningfully, then turned and led their horses up the spongy slope. They tied their horses in a dense stand of mixed conifers, removed their Winchesters from their saddle boots, then crept back down the grade, until they could see the sun-dappled trail thirty yards away.

They sat smoking, the breeze blowing the smoke out behind them. After about fifteen minutes, they heard a sharp clack, like a horse kicking a rock, then a creaking saddle. One at a time, they quietly levered shells into the breeches of their Winchesters.

They sat there, rifles on their knees, until the rider appeared on their left, coming along the trail below them. He was a medium tall man in a cowhide vest and black felt hat with a dented crown. Sun dappled the crown, making it glow. A tin star winked on his vest.

He'd ridden about fifteen more feet when he suddenly reined his sorrel quarterhorse to a halt and jerked a look to his right, toward Beach and Gruber. Sighting down the barrel resting on his knee, Gruber squeezed the trigger, the rifle cracking and bouncing with the report. The man with the star flew off the left side of his horse and rolled down the slope. The horse gave a whinny and bounded off its hind legs, hightailing up the trail.

Gruber looked at Beach with a contained grin. Then both men stood and walked down the slope, Beach holding his rifle cautiously out before him, Gruber holding his casually down at his side, an arrogant set to his mouth.

They found the man about twenty feet from the trail, lying facedown between two pines, blood smudged in the leaves and needles he'd churned up as he'd rolled. He lay at an odd angle, his left arm pinned beneath him, hatless head turned sideways, blood dribbling from a jagged cut on his chin, another on his brow.

"That McCreedy?" Beach asked.

"I don't know," Gruber said, rolling the man onto his back.

Gruber heard the two quick reports about the same time he saw the man lift his left hand and extend the gun, which sent blades of smoke and fire first into Gruber, then into Beach. Gruber twisted around and hit the ground chest down, his face buried in leaves and the sharp tang of pine resin. He'd just realized what had happened, when everything went black.

Owen McCreedy lay on his hip, gun extended, staring at the two men, making sure they were dead, and listening, wondering if the gunfire had been heard by the rest of Brown's army, wondering if Brown had sent out more pickets.

When he was sure both men were dead, and relatively sure no others were in the immediate vicinity, he looked at his bloody right arm, feeling as though a hot poker had plunged all the way to the bone. He holstered his pistol, reached around with his left hand, and tore his right sleeve down to his elbow, revealing the bloody hole.

Cursing the pain, he then removed his neckerchief, and wrapped and tied it around the wound, hoping the wrap would stop the bleeding. He knew he should go back to town and get the arm tended by a doctor, but he couldn't turn back now. Brown and his men were headed after Prophet and the girl. McCreedy knew it now without a doubt. Who else would they be after out here, and why else would Brown have sent out pickets to ambush trackers?

While he'd figured out who they were after, McCreedy couldn't figure out where they were going. The trail they were following led to Miner's Gulch. How would they have gotten Prophet trapped in there? But if they had, Prophet was going to need all the help he could get.

With that urgent thought propelling him forward, McCreedy gained his feet. Holding his throbbing arm, he climbed the hill to the trail and started walking in the direction of his horse, finding the animal twenty minutes later, grazing the sun-dappled meadow near the trail. The horse belonged to Perry Moon, but the animal knew McCreedy, and didn't run as the sheriff approached, talking to the animal as gently as he could considering the pain he was in, as well as the hurry.

Mounting up with a painful sigh, wagging his head against the hot throbs piercing his core, he gigged the horse into a trot, keeping his eyes peeled on both sides of the trail so he wouldn't get shot out of his saddle again. As he rode, he reached back and shucked his Winchester with his good arm, knowing he'd need it soon.

22

PROPHET SQUATTED ON a butte top, one hand on his Winchester, and smoked a cigarette. The sun was high, almost straight up, and his sweated collar stuck to his unshaven neck.

Below him lay the rocky floor of Miner's Gulch. Harsh sunlight speckled the unnamed creek snaking through the scattered mix of conifers and deciduous trees. It coursed around the back of the old cabin Prophet remembered from his short stay in the country five years ago.

He watched the long-abandoned hovel—weathered gray, doorless, no window glass, battered chimney pipe— and felt his heart beat rhythmically beneath his sternum. Things would be happening soon now . . . very soon. Prophet would at last meet the bottom-feeder who'd sent his firebrands out to kill him and Lola but who'd managed instead to kill a coach load of innocent stage passengers—a boy, two old people, and good ole Mike Clatsop to boot.

Obviously, that was how Billy Brown worked. He gave the word, and whomever he wanted dead was a target—never mind the cost. Sometimes he even did the killing himself, as had been the case with Hoyt Farley, which told Prophet the man didn't mind getting his own hands dirty now and then. That's why Prophet believed Billy himself would show today, along with his entire army. Billy wouldn't want to risk letting Prophet and the girl slip away. They'd no doubt become quite the thorns in his hide.

Prophet smiled at that thought, enjoying what little comfort he could take from the situation. But then, too, there had been Lola last night, naked in his arms. . . . He couldn't get his mind off of her this morning, no matter how hard he tried to concentrate on the matter at hand. Maybe he'd slept with whores too long. It had been a long time since he'd made love like that . . . been made love to like that . . . with that kind of passion.

It was almost as though they'd both been expecting to die today. . . .

The feel of her writhing beneath him faded reluctantly when a magpie threw up an alarm, bounding out of a pine branch west of the cabin. Prophet cast his gaze that way, hunkering low and fingering the Winchester.

Through the trembling leaves he spied riders, saw only glimpses of horses and men spreading out in the woods before the cabin. Movement behind the cabin attracted Prophet's eye. More riders appeared there, moving out from the aspens and splashing across the creek, rifles held across their saddles, hats tilted over their foreheads. They wore cream dusters and their faces were brown ovals beneath their hat brims.

When they'd fanned out around the cabin, dismounting and taking cover behind the rocks along the stream, three men rode into the clearing before the cabin. One was squat and wearing a suit beneath his duster, and a derby hat. A gold watch chain winked in the sunlight. The man riding beside him was of medium height and broad-shouldered. The third wore long red hair down his back, and an ostentatious mustache and beard.

The squat man held his rifle butt down on his thigh and gave his gaze to the cabin. "Hello the camp! Prophet, you in there?"

Prophet's heart picked up its rhythm.

"Prophet, you in there?" the squat man asked again, barking it loudly, angrily. That had to be Billy—ornery little bulldog of a gussied-up thug.

Prophet got to his feet and extended his rifle out before him, aiming. He didn't want to kill Billy. Not yet. He'd save the crime boss for later, when he was staring him in the eye.

The gun barked.

In the canyon, Billy Brown jerked his head around sharply as a bullet smacked the head of the man riding beside him. A small round hole appeared about two inches before the man's right ear, in the shade of his hat. The man sat there for a moment, swaying in the saddle, making wet, sighing sounds. He held tightly to his reins. Gradually, the grip loosened, his hands opened, and the man fell sideways out of his saddle.

"What the *hell*!" Billy cried, jerking his head around.

Prophet extended his rifle above his head and waved it. "Up here, Billy. Come and get me, you son of a bitch!"

He pivoted, jogged down the other side of the butte, and jumped onto his horse tied to a shrub. Holding his rifle in one hand, he reached out to untie the reins with the other, then gigged the horse up a winding trail in the butte behind him, his heart pounding, adrenaline spurting in his veins.

Down in Miner's Gulch, Billy stared at the butte top which Prophet had just vacated. His eyes were like daggers, his mouth set with exasperation. "Get after that son of a bitch!" he ordered in his high, raspy tenor, which cracked a little on the end note. He stabbed his horse with his spurs, and the animal lunged off its hindquarters.

"I'm not sure that's a good idea, Boss," Clive Russo warned behind him. "That's just what he wants us to do."

"Ride, you cream puff!"

Russo shook his head as he watched the others fall in behind Billy, whose horse pounded through the clearing, into the woods and up the southern butte. Reluctantly, knowing he had no choice in the matter, the *segundo* joined them, galloping to catch up with his boss.

When Prophet had crested another ridge, he quickly dismounted and squatted down on his haunches, bringing the Winchester up to his shoulder. He waited, hearing Brown's men galloping up the escarpment just north of him, the pounding of the hooves and the clinking of rein chains and bits growing louder.

When Prophet saw the first two riders cresting the ridge, he aimed and quickly fired, pausing to watch the one on the right roll backwards off his horse. Prophet shot the other man just as he jerked a look at his fallen pard. The man fell to the right, got his right boot caught in the stirrup, and was dragged to the bottom of the escarpment before being deposited in a juniper shrub.

Billy Brown rode up behind the first fallen man, raising his rifle to fire at the opposite ridge. He scowled, mouth bunching, eyes narrowing, looking around.

No one was there.

He lowered the rifle and waved an arm. "Come on, you sorry bastards! After that son of a bitch!"

Behind him, riding parallel with two other galloping riders, Clive Russo quirted his horse and shook his head. He had one hell of a bad case of the jitters. . . .

As Prophet galloped his mount down the ridge and reined him westward through a narrow gorge, the bounty man thought, *Three down, twenty-two to go.*

He repeated the refrain over and over as he left the gorge, hung a sharp right, and gigged his horse through a valley, hoping both that Brown's men hadn't lost him in that gorge and that they didn't gain on him too quickly. They had the advantage of riding horses they'd probably ridden for a couple of years and knew better than they knew each other. In contrast, Prophet was riding a horse he'd ridden for only a couple of days. The gelding seemed to have a good set of lungs, and so far he'd been surefooted, but it would only take one misstep on this treacherous terrain to smoke Prophet's hide for sure.

Crossing a saddle, he reined the horse to the left and saw Silver Canyon open before him, its toothy ridges looming impressively at least a quarter mile over the rock-strewn canyon floor. When he came to the trail that had been carved by deer and mountain goats, he gritted his teeth and reined the horse to the right, spurring it up the mountain, weaving between towering gray boulders and clattering over shale.

"Come on, horse . . . gidup!" Prophet rasped, holding the reins loose in his hands, elbows rising and falling like wings. The horse was breathing hard and saliva streaked from its lips, but it was lunging off its hindquarters like a pro, as though it had been bred for these very peaks.

"Come on . . . come on . . . !"

Three-quarters up the switchbacking trail, Prophet brought the horse to a halt and looked down. Brown's men were just now riding into the canyon, dusters flapping behind them in the wind. When they did not see

Prophet on the trail ahead, and had lost his tracks, they slowed and milled along the canyon floor, looking around. Several men raised their heads and spied Prophet at the same time. They jutted their arms out, pointing.

"There!"

Prophet jerked a look up the ridge above him, to a nest of rocks he recognized. "Okay, Lola, now, now, now!" he shouted.

Before the last word, he heard the booming report of Dick Dunbar's Big Fifty. It sounded like one of the Howitzers that had thrown grapeshot at him during the War Between the States, and it made the hair stand on the back of his neck. It was not an unwelcome sound, however. With each boom resounding off the canyon walls, he clucked to his horse, and grinned, continuing up the wall toward the peak.

Boom! sounded the gun. Then, after the five seconds it took Lola to reload the singleshot beast . . . *boom!*

He was only about thirty yards from the ridge when he heard a rumbling, as though from a distant storm. He checked his horse down to a stop, and twisted around in his saddle, giving his gaze to the men behind him. The Big Fifty's shots had slowed them down, and they were scattered along the mountain below him, looking frantically around, rifle butts on their thighs, their horses slipping in the loose gravel. Hearing the rumbling, several looked behind them, at the opposite canyon wall.

Panting, Prophet grinned as the rumbling grew in volume until it sounded like the thunderhead was careening over the canyon with a vengeance. The ground vibrated, and Prophet felt his own bones resounding like a tuning fork.

He glanced at the opposite wall as several boulders, prompted by the Big Fifty's probing balls and cannonlike booms, peeled loose from their precarious moorings. As if slowed down somehow, they tumbled downward, smashing others as they went, starting the rockslide Prophet had once been so afraid of and now welcomed like rain after a long drought.

Prophet gave a rebel yell as he crested the ridge.

Hunkered in the nest of rocks, where Prophet had deposited her earlier, the showgirl snugged her cheek up to the gun's heavy stock once more and squeezed the trigger. The gun flashed and boomed, bucking like a horse, throwing her into the rock behind her and nearly bouncing out of her grasp.

Unfazed by the tumult, she turned her head up at Prophet and grinned.

"That's some fancy shootin' for a showgirl!" he whooped, casting his gaze back down the canyon.

The floor was a pillow of billowing gray dust. The roar was deafening and the ground shook as though it were about to crack and heave like a California quake.

Prophet tossed his reins to Lola and dismounted, walking to the lip of the ridge. He stared down, rifle in his hands. The cries of the men and horses, crushed by the falling rock, rose on the resounding roars. Gritting his teeth, fingering his rifle and listening, Prophet waited.

He didn't have to wait long. Two riders, managing to ride clear of the slide, appeared simultaneously out of the dust. Prophet knelt, took aim, and fired. The man left his saddle with his arms splayed, landing in the jumbled rocks around him. His horse turned and reared, giving a loud, ear-piercing whinny.

Prophet fired at the other man, who crouched at the last second, dodging the slug. Prophet jacked another round into the chamber, but before he could aim again, two more riders appeared out of the billowing dust, teeth gritted, eyes black as kill-crazy grizzlies.

Turning, Prophet said to Lola, "Mount up!" and

climbed onto his own sweat-lathered horse.

Turning back toward the charging riders, Prophet lifted the Winchester and fired, covering Lola as she ran several yards down the mountain's backside and mounted her horse waiting for her under a wind-torn conifer. When she was in the saddle, Prophet gigged his own horse out ahead of her, leading the way down the mountain, through the tall pines peppered with aspens and box elders.

As they rode, the bullets zinging around them and thunking into trees told Prophet that at least a handful of Brown's men had survived the landslide. They'd crested the ridge, and were now galloping behind them, probably about fifty or sixty yards away—well within Winchester range.

When they reached the bottom of the mountain and had splashed across a shallow creek, Prophet halted his horse and turned to Lola. "Okay, just like we planned now! Keep riding!"

Her horse facing him sideways, Lola stared at him from beneath the brim of her straw hat, wincing as though in physical pain. "You be careful, Lou!"

"I will! Now ride!"

She reined her horse around and heeled him into a gallop along the stream, disappearing into woods about fifty yards away. Prophet turned his horse behind a knoll, dismounted, and ground-staked the reins. Winchester in hand, he crawled to the top of the knoll, jacked a shell in the breech, and fired just as three riders appeared in the clearing at the base of the mountain.

The man on the left leaned back in the saddle, a hole through his forehead, while his horse rode past Prophet and continued downstream at a gallop. The others were sawing back on their reins, aware of the ambush. Prophet squeezed the Winchester's trigger and unsaddled a rail-thin man with with a scraggly beard. The riderless horse followed the first downstream.

Prophet jacked another shell and slid a gaze around the crest of the knoll. All he saw was woods and the vague outline of a horse and one leg of its rider, hidden behind a tree.

"Prophet, goddamnit, you double-crosser!"

Prophet knew the raspy shriek belonged to Billy Brown.

"Rode right into it, too, didn't you, stupid bastard." Prophet laughed.

"Where's the girl?"

"Long gone. Just you and me now, Billy."

"I still have three men left, Prophet. And we're gonna fill you so full of holes your own mother won't recognize you."

Prophet was about to respond when guns opened up from the woods, smoke puffing from under the pines. At the same time, the man in the bowler hat bounded out from behind a thick-trunked tree, shooting a pistol in Prophet's direction, and galloped his horse downstream.

Jerking his head back behind the knoll, the bounty hunter wheezed a curse. Brown was going after Lola while these other three men pinned Prophet down.

Prophet jerked his rifle around the knoll and squeeze off two quick shots before the hammer fell benignly against the firing pin. Empty.

Shit!

Wanting to get after Lola as quickly as he could and frantically thumbing shells out of his cartridge belt and into his rifle's receiver, Prophet heard the gunfire and the slugs tearing into the mound behind him, throwing up chunks of dirt, pebbles, and sod.

"He's empty," someone called. "Storm him!"

Prophet's heart danced and his fingers shook as he

thumbed the cartridges through the receiver's door. One slipped out of his sweaty fingers. Hearing horses pounding around him, he bent to retrieve it, blew the dust off the brass casing, and slipped it into the breech.

The pounding of the hooves was all around him. . . .

Turning to face the woods and scrambling atop the knoll, he jacked a shell in the chamber of his rifle and clawed his pistol off his hip. Two riders bounded toward him, firing their rifles. Prophet blew one off his horse with the Winchester, and shot the other man twice in the chest with his Colt. Knowing that one more lingered in the trees, Prophet ran that way, between the two riderless horses coming to a harried halt and pivoting to run in opposite directions.

Smoke puffed from the woods. Keying on it, Prophet dropped to a knee and cut loose with his Winchester, levering one shell after another. He'd fired all eight rounds when a dry voice rose.

"All right. All right. I give up. My guns are empty."

"Step out here, you bastard."

A man stepped out from behind a pine. Surrendering, he raised his pistol in one hand, rifle in the other. He was the man Prophet had seen earlier, with long red hair and Custer-style mustache. He stared at Prophet dully. Then his impudent mouth lifted a grin. Prophet raised his pistol and blew a hole through the man's chest, sending him backwards into the woods, blood spurting through his expensive wool vest and black cravat.

"Never shoulda smiled like that," Prophet grumbled as he wheeled and ran behind the knoll for his horse. Forking leather, he kicked the mount into a gallop, heading upstream toward Billy Brown and Lola, his fear for her safety spreading like a cancer throughout his loins. . . .

23

LOLA RODE HARD, but her heart wasn't in it. Gunfire cracked behind her. She was so worried about Prophet that she felt as though each crack sent a bullet through her spine.

After about a mile, she halted her horse along the stream she'd followed onto a grassy saddle bordered by buttes. She turned her horse around and stared tensely back the way she'd come, hoping she'd see Prophet riding toward her. Against her better judgment, she'd fallen head-over-heels in love with the strapping Southerner, and she shuddered at the thought of Brown's gunslicks killing him.

Finally, she saw someone galloping toward her along the stream. Her heart lifted expectantly, and her gaze intensified. When the rider was a hundred yards away, a shudder ran through her. Her heart grew heavy, her stomach cold. The rider was not Prophet. His short stature, wide shoulders, watch fob, and gray head—apparently, he'd lost his hat in the fracas—bespoke Billy Brown!

Lola gave an involuntary scream and jerked her horse around, then spurred him into a gallop up the trail. She went fifty yards, until the stream curved into a foliage-choked gorge. Halting, she swung her frantic gaze around, then took a game trail into a narrow valley. Looking behind, she saw the rider closing in, head lowered against the wind, arm winging as he slapped his horse's rump.

"No!" Lola screamed, turning her head back to the trail.

Leaves and branches swiped at her from both sides. She had no idea where she was or where she had gotten off the trail Prophet had told her to take. At the moment, she only cared that she stay ahead of Billy Brown.

Turning a corner in the trail, she got an idea. She looked behind her and heard the hooves of Brown's mount. Quickly, she twisted the reins to the left and urged the horse up the wooded mountain slope. She hoped to lose Billy here, in the dense brush and fallen logs. The going was slow, however—much slower than she'd anticipated. The horse was winded and the blow-down trees brought it to complete stops before it bounded halfheartedly over each, blowing raucously, spittle string-ing from its nostrils.

On the open ridge, she stopped to rest the horse. Look-ing back the way she'd come, she saw and heard nothing until a pistol cracked. She gave a start, her face turning gray, eyes widening with fear. The gun cracked again, the slug clipping a branch only two feet from her head. The horse whinnied, and, tired as it was, reared several feet in the air, turning away from the noise.

Heart beating an Indian war dance in her chest, Lola gave the horse its head, and the animal plunged down a steep mountain grade covered with talus. The horse went down on its knees several times, Lola hanging for dear life to the horn, gritting her teeth and squeezing her eyes closed. Just before bottoming out on the valley floor, she swept her gaze back up the mountain and turned deathly chill at the sight of Billy Brown sitting his stationary mount, aiming a pistol at her.

She heard the bullet zing past her ear a half second before the report.

"No!" she cried as the horse came to the bottom of the grade. "*Go, go!*" she urged.

The horse clopped and splashed across a stream, a weathered-gray cabin appearing on her right. Wasn't this the cabin Prophet had shown her earlier in the morning, when they'd been planning their attack and escape routes?

It was a fleeting consideration, since it did nothing to help her escape Brown now, who was thundering down the mountain and gaining several feet on her with every lunge of his stallion. Lola ducked under an aspen bough, aimed her horse down the trail hugging the stream, and heeled it hard, slapping its rump with her left hand. She tossed a look over her shoulder and was not surprised to see the stout, suited man behind her, watch chain flopping across his vested belly, gaining enough ground that Lola could see the fiendish grin stretching his lips.

He extended his pistol toward her and squeezed off another shot. Instinctively, Lola ducked her head and turned back to the trail streaming beneath her, feeling her heart shrink and her pulse slow as she neared the end. Prophet was no doubt dead, and soon she would be, as well. . . .

Behind her, Brown slapped his horse's rump with one hand and squeezed his gun and reins with the other. He grinned as he watched the horse and girl grow closer,

getting larger and larger as his stout stallion shrank the
ground between them. He only had one bullet left in his
gun, so he wanted to make sure he sent it home—either
into the horse or the girl herself. Either way, the girl
would die. . . .

As he neared the left rear of the girl's horse, he eased
his gun arm out before him, carefully aiming the pistol.
He thought he could plug the girl through her head at
this range—the trail was fairly straight, his gun hand
moving with his horse's stride.

Thumbing back the hammer, he started increasing the
tension on the trigger. He stopped, frowning with surprise, when a man suddenly appeared along the trail, to
Brown's left. He was holding something out from his
body, like a club. Billy didn't have time to identify the
object before it smacked his face so hard he felt his lips
and teeth break. Before he knew what had happened, he
was sailing ass-over-head backwards off his saddle.

Owen McCreedy stood holding his rifle by the barrel
and gazing down at the half-conscious Brown. Billy lay
facedown in the grass along the trail, moaning as he
rolled slightly from side to side, his face in his hands.
Even though his wounded arm throbbed mercilessly,
McCreedy grinned. He had the son of a bitch. He finally
had him. He knew it wasn't a very professional senti-
ment, but boy had smacking that man in the mug felt
good!

Hooves thumped behind him. He turned to watch the
girl ride toward him, a cautious set to her face. He raised
a placating hand. "It's all right, miss. I'm Owen Mc-
Creedy, sheriff of Johnson City."

"How," she said, shaking her head, "how did you find
us here?"

McCreedy winced from the pain in his arm. Before he
could reply, Lola shook her head again, as though to

nullify her question. "Lou needs help," she said urgently. "They have him pinned down back there, about two miles!"

"Shit," McCreedy said, exhaling and staring down at Brown, a pained expression on his face. "Okay, I tell you what we do," he told her. "You stay here with him. You have a gun?"

She nodded and patted the rifle boot housing the Sharp's on the other side of her Appaloosa.

"All right—I'll get my horse," he said, turning and starting for the aspen grove behind him.

He hadn't walked more than ten feet, when Lola said sharply, "Wait!"

McCreedy turned to her. "What is it?"

She pointed back the way she'd come. "Someone's coming."

McCreedy turned. Sure enough, a lone rider was approaching at a gallop. McCreedy brought the rifle to his chest, but checked himself. The man came on, but seeing them, he slowed to a canter.

"It's him!" Lola fairly screamed. "It's Lou!"

She gigged her horse out to meet him. McCreedy watched as the two came together, the girl throwing herself around Prophet's neck and Prophet doing nothing to discourage the attention. McCreedy gave his head a shake.

That dog . . .

At length, the girl turned her horse around and followed Prophet, who approached McCreedy with his trademark shit-eating grin, cantering his horse sideways and checking him down when he was about ten feet away. "Howdy, Owen," he said, noticing the sheriff's bloody arm and frowning. "What in the hell are you doing out here?"

"I followed Billy and his thugs out from town," the

sheriff said, lowering his gaze to Brown, who had crawled onto his hands and knees, spitting blood and teeth in the grass. "They bushwacked me about three miles back."

"I see that," Prophet said. "You're gonna need some attention there."

"So's he," McCreedy said, regarding the thug with a grin. To Prophet, he said, "What about the others?"

"Dead."

McCreedy was incredulous. "All?"

Prophet turned to Lola and smiled. "Never turn your back on a girl and a Sharp's Big Fifty, Owen."

Brown lifted his enraged eyes to Prophet and cursed. The bounty hunter could only tell from the tone it was a curse, for the man's mouth was so full of broken teeth and blood, his speech was garbled.

Brown jabbed a finger at McCreedy and gummed several more unintelligible phrases. "Save it, Billy," McCreedy said, reaching down with his one good hand and jerking the man to his feet. "Save it for the trial." He looked at Lola. "You'll testify?"

Lola gave an unequivocal nod, glaring hot hate at the crime boss, who returned her stare. Her voice was steel. "Sheriff, I'll testify to him slashing Hoyt Farley's throat while his gunslicks held the poor man's arms"—she swung her confident gaze to McCreedy—"and to a whole lot more."

"Okay," McCreedy said, nodding. He turned to Prophet. "Let's get this son of a bitch on a horse and haul him off to the hoosegow . . . and a hangman's noose."

24

TWO WEEKS LATER, in his big, canopied bed in the Nuremberg, Prophet rolled over to wrap Lola in his arms. He got an armload of pillow instead. Groggily lifting his head, hair mussed and eyes narrowed, he looked around the room lit by golden morning rays slanting through the thin, crocheted curtains.

He turned to the dressing room. "Lola?"

No response. He hadn't really expected any. The door was open, and he could see she wasn't there. Casting another glance around the room, he saw that all her clothes, recently purchased over the past two weeks in Johnson City, and which, during their lovemaking, had been strewn about the carpeted floor, were gone. Gone, also, were the new carpetbag and portmanteau she'd bought for traveling.

Planting his elbows on the bed and running his hands through his hair, he heard the words she'd whispered the other night, as they lay entangled in the darkened room. "One of these mornings I'm going to wake up and go— okay, Lou?" she'd said.

"What?"

"It'll be easier that way."

He'd looked at her, baffled.

She pressed her cheek to his chest. When she spoke, her voice was small and far away, like a little girl's. "Let's not pretend this is anything more than what it is."

"What is it?"

She shrugged her naked shoulders. He could feel the warmth and wetness of her lips on his chest. "A fling. A wonderful, wonderful fling . . ."

He'd sighed. She was right. How could they be anything more than what they were right now? She was a showgirl aiming for the big time. A man would only stand in her way. He was a reclusive bounty hunter, bound to the mountains and plains, the wild places in the West, a saddle tramp more at home atop a horse than even a saloon chair.

Her shoulders jerked twice. The spreading wetness on his chest was tears. He ran his hands slowly up and down her narrow back and supple hips. She pushed herself onto her hands and knees, and straddled him, gazing smokily into his eyes. Slowly, and for one of their last times, their most passionate time ever, they made love. . . .

Now he rolled out of bed with a sigh, feeling hollow and lethargic, and climbed into a new pair of denims. He shaved at the commode stand. He wet his hair down and combed it, then shrugged into the shirt she'd picked out for him at the dry-goods store—a soft chambray with red piping. Everything they'd bought had been on the expense account Owen McCreedy had arranged for them, tapped directly from Billy Brown's assets, in payment for all they'd gone through getting here.

Prophet didn't mind taking the handout, since it was Brown's money. Brown sure didn't need it. The town had hanged him two days ago, and sent his disbarred attorney packing. They'd had a street dance afterward.

When he'd buttoned the shirt and stomped into his boots, he packed his saddlebags, draped them over his shoulder, and headed downstairs, lighting a cigarette. He felt distracted and lonely and just plain sad. The carpeted lobby was too bright for his mood. Sourly, he paid his bill but managed a feeble wink when thanking the porter for the extra attention—food and drink at all hours, extra pillows and baths. He slipped a gold eagle into the lad's shirt pocket, and headed outside.

Looking to his left, he saw the morning stage to Cheyenne sitting outside the station, passengers milling near its open door. Lola stood near the rear, watching the driver load her bags into the boot. She looked lovely in her new blue traveling dress and feathered hat which contrasted with the red of her hair. She carried a ruffled parasol in one hand and a smartly beaded reticule in the other. As though she felt his gaze, she turned his way, and crossed her hands before her.

He adjusted the saddlebags on his shoulder and, puffing his cigarette, strolled across the street. She smiled as he approached, and inclined her head. "You're going to make this hard for me, aren't you?"

He shrugged. "Just wanted to say good-bye, that's all."

"I hate good-byes."

He let the saddlebags fall down his arm and into the dust at his feet. He took his cigarette in his right hand, stepped forward, and engulfed her in his arms. He held her tightly for a long time, sniffing her neck. He smiled.

He held her at arm's length to gaze into her eyes. "We had one hell of a ride, didn't we?"

Her eyes were veiled with tears, but she was smiling.

She nodded. "I had a wonderful time with you, you big lout. Even when things were looking desperate. But it's all over now." She gazed up the street, where several men were slowly dismantling the gallows from which Billy Brown had been hung. "I could stay another week, but why? We have to part sometime."

Prophet nodded. "Headin' for Denver?"

She nodded.

He squinted at her. "Good luck to you, Miss Diamond."

She threw herself into his arms and kissed him. Her lips were full and supple; they clung to him for several seconds.

"Good-bye, Lou. I'll never forget you."

"I couldn't forget you if I tried, Lola."

"All aboard, ma'am," the driver said.

She glanced at Prophet once more, then turned to the stage, lifting her skirts as the driver helped her board. When the door closed, and the driver climbed up to the box, Prophet stepped forward and said through the window, "Hey, you never told me your real name."

She looked at him, giving a defiant smile. "And I never will, either."

Prophet chuckled as the driver yelled at the horses and the stage jerked away. When it was halfway down the block, steering through the crowd of horseback riders and wagons, Lola poked her head out the window, looking back at him.

"It's Margaret Jane Olson," she yelled.

Prophet walked forward, cupping his ear. "What is it?"

"Margaret Jane Olson, and don't you dare tell a soul!" She watched him, smiling brightly. She threw him a kiss. Then the dust thickened between them. She waved, the stage turned a corner, and she was gone.

Prophet stuck his cigarette between his lips and stared

after the thinning dust plume, swallowing a dry knot in his throat. "Good luck, Margaret Jane," he said, exhaling smoke.

"Too bad," someone said behind him. "She's as pretty as a Georgia sunset."

Prophet turned to see Owen McCreedy standing in the shade outside the sheriff's office, his left arm in a sling.

"You noticed, did you? What would Alice think?"

The sheriff grinned and shrugged his shoulders. "Alice ain't here. She's home making a rhubarb pie. I was about to head that way for another cup of coffee and a slice of that pie. Join me?"

"Nah," Prophet said, feeling churlish, wanting a drink.

"Might cheer you up," McCreedy said enticingly. "Besides, I figure I owe you a piece of rhubarb pie—your favorite, ain't it?—after nearly getting you killed. Again, I sure am sorry about that, Proph. I guess I underestimated the length of ole Billy's tentacles."

"Wasn't your fault, Owen. Someone got word to him that you found the girl—that's all."

"Yeah, but who the hell could that have been? The only ones who knew were you, me, Perry Moon, the sheriff who found her in the first place, and Sheriff Fitzsimmons up to Henry's Crossing. I didn't tell another soul."

Prophet had been studying the dust at his feet. Now he turned his gaze to McCreedy, a dim light in his eyes, as though a thought had just occurred to him. At length, he stopped to pick up his saddlebags.

"Well, I'll take my rifle and shotgun off your hands now, Owen," he said. He'd left both weapons with the sheriff for safekeeping.

"That mean your declining my offer of a slice of Alice's pie?" McCreedy asked as he stepped inside the jail.

"I reckon I'll be headin' back up to Johnson City," Prophet said behind him.

When the sheriff appeared in the doorway with his shotgun and Winchester, Prophet laid the barrels of both across his shoulder.

"What business do you have up in Johnson City?" McCreedy asked with a probing gaze.

"I left my ugly horse up there," Prophet said. "I better get him back before someone shoots the son of a bitch." He turned and started for the livery barn, where he'd stabled the horse he'd borrowed from old man Hill at the Backwater station.

"Hey," McCreedy called after him, "you don't think Fitzsimmons let the cat out of the bag, do you?"

"Little Fitz?" Prophet said, feigning surprise as he half-turned toward the sheriff. "That walking, talking, star-toting symbol of rock-hard justice?" Prophet turned and continued toward the livery barn. "Not a chance."

It was a lonely, uneventful ride to Henry's Crossing, and Prophet spent most of the trip feeling sorry for himself and missing Lola. Never before had he known nights so long and quiet, the sky so full of stars twinkling mockingly far above—millions of miles away and no one to share them with. No Lola to skinny-dip with and make love to.

Lordy, how a woman could infect a man's mind. He felt heavy and dismal.

"You gotta get out of this rut," he told himself. "You need another job."

He decided to start perusing wanted dodgers once he'd taken care of his business in Henry's Crossing.

To that end, he rode down the little river berg's main street four days after leaving Johnson City. Amid the din of passing freighters, their dry wheels creaking and mules

braying, Prophet rode up to the livery barn where he'd
stabled his ornery hammerhead, Mean and Ugly. He arranged for a boy to return the horse he'd borrowed from
old man Hill at the Backwater station, with a twenty-five-
dollar token of appreciation, and sprung Mean and Ugly,
who'd become sleek off all the oats he'd been fed, but
was as mean and ugly as ever. He took several nips out
of Prophet's arm as the bounty hunter saddled him and
strapped his soogan behind the saddle.

The horse even bucked a couple times on the way over
to the sheriff's office. "So that's what it's gonna be,
huh?" Prophet said with disgust, wrapping the reins
around the hitching post. "Well, we'll see about that."

He turned and knocked on the office door.

"It's open!" came the sharp reply.

Prophet stepped inside and closed the door behind him.
He looked at Fitzsimmons, who sat behind his desk, all
decked out in a new black suit with wool vest and gold
watch fob. The slouch hat tipped back on his head was
new, as well—crisp as a newly minted coin. The gun
snugged on the sheriff's scrawny hip was silver-plated
and factory engraved, the grips mother of pearl. The holster was hand-tooled. It looked as though it had just been
sewn. It was one of those break-away contraptions favored by gunslicks.

Prophet whistled. "Well, well . . . look at you."

Fitzsimmons flushed. He was in the middle of his din-
ner, a china plate containing a T-bone steak, greens, and
baked potato on the desk before him. A checked napkin
was draped over a knee. When he'd seen Prophet, his
fork had froze halfway to his mouth, a new ring winking
on his pinky.

"You musta hit the mother lode!" Prophet cried, shaking his head and running his eyes up and down the sheriff's new duds.

Fitzsimmons studied Prophet sourly, eyes befuddled. He worked his mouth, his gray, upswept mustache moving back and forth. "Where in the hell did you come from?"

"Surprised to see me, Fitz?"

"Well . . . I . . . I—"

"No doubt you are, since you sold me and Lola out to Billy Brown."

Suddenly, the blood ran out of Fitzsimmons's face, like water through a sieve. He set his fork on his plate. "What . . . what are you talkin' about?"

"I'm talkin' about you tellin' Brown's man that McCreedy sent me after the girl." Prophet dropped into a chair before the sheriff's desk. "I figure some of Brown's riders happened by one day—maybe Mr. Bannon himself—lookin' for the girl, and told you he'd set you up right sweet if you gave him a whistle if you saw her. Ain't that how it worked?"

Fitzsimmons came half out of his chair, bristling. "I did no such—"

"Then how did the man who hopped the stage with us know she and I were here? The only people who knew were McCreedy, his deputy, the sheriff who found her in the first place, Lola, myself . . . and you."

The sheriff opened his mouth to protest. Prophet stopped him.

"Now, I know McCreedy didn't do it. Neither Lola nor I did. I met Perry Moon, and that kid wouldn't tell a lie to save to his soul. I've never met the sheriff who told McCreedy about seeing the girl passing through his town, but it just plum don't make sense that he would have told McCreedy *and* Brown. So that just leaves you, Fitz."

The sheriff sat slowly back in his chair, staring at

Prophet guiltily. His mouth worked, but no words came out. Sweat beaded his forehead.

"Innocent people died because of you, Fitz," Prophet said. "For that, you should be hung."

Prophet let the words hang in the five feet of dry air between them. The sheriff bowed his head to look at his hands. Suddenly, he convulsed in a sob.

"He set you up right well, I see," Prophet continued. "You buy your wife a new outfit, too? Maybe do some work on the house?"

Fitzsimmons lifted his gaze to Prophet. His eyes were angry. "You don't know what it's like, workin' for this town. No one takes me serious. They laugh 'cause I'm old. Don't think I'm worth a dime, so they hardly pay me a damn thing."

Prophet didn't say anything. His chest rose and fell angrily, remembering the burning stage.

Haltingly, Fitzsimmons said, "So . . . yeah . . . when Brown's men came to town lookin' for the girl, I told 'em. Hell, I didn't know what was goin' on. I didn't know they were gonna try to kill her."

"But you had to suspect as much. You didn't care if they killed me."

Fitzsimmons's nose wrinkled and he turned away. There was a long silence, Fitzsimmons staring at the wall, Prophet staring at Fitzsimmons.

"Well, I suppose you're gonna tell the council . . . have me fired and put away," the old sheriff said with a sigh.

Prophet considered this. He knew that's what he should do. Innocent people had died because of the old sot. But then, ruining Fitzsimmons, who really couldn't have known what the effects of his transgressions would be, wouldn't bring those people back. And why put the old bastard's long-suffering wife through even more?

"Here's what I'm gonna do, Fitz," Prophet said at last,

getting out his making sack and producing a paper. "I'm gonna keep my mouth shut if you do two things."

He glanced at the hawk-nosed old man as he drew a line of tobacco across the paper. The sheriff didn't say anything, but watched him with a mix of derision and expectation.

"First," Prophet said, "I want you to donate a hundred dollars to the Queen Bee. Give the hundred to Miss Angie. She'll spread it around to the other girls equally without saying anything to the madam."

He was working the paper around the tobacco. Fitzsimmons's cheeks were bunched, his lips pursed, scowling.

"Then," Prophet continued, "I want you to donate another hundred to those three orphans working over at the Mulligan Stew." Fitzsimmons began breathing heavily through his nose, face flushing again. Prophet ignored him. "Spread it out evenly. Make sure each kid gets his fair share. They get paid peanuts over there, if that." He twisted the ends of the cigarette and stuck the quirley between his lips. "Sound good?"

Fitzsimmons climbed halfway out of his chair and pounded a fist on his desk. "Two hundred and fifty is all Brown gave me in the first place!"

"Then it almost works out perfectly, doesn't it?" Prophet said, smiling grandly. He scratched a lucifer on the desk and touched it to the cigarette, inhaling deeply.

Fitzsimmons crouched there, washed-out eyes bright with hate. Prophet thought his swelling nose would explode.

"You do it, Fitz," Prophet warned. "I'm gonna talk to Miss Angie and those three orphans next time I'm in town. If you don't, I'll not only thrash the shit out of you, I'll go to the city council and spill the beans—the whole pot."

He gave the sheriff a wink. Then he climbed to his feet and started for the door, hearing the sheriff rasping heavily, hatefully behind him.

On his way to the door, Prophet stopped. A dodger on the bulletin board had caught his eye. He moved toward it, squinting his eyes. "Five hundred dollars—dead or alive," he read aloud, with a thoughtful air.

He plucked the dodger off the board and turned to the sheriff sitting back in his chair, looking as though the sky had just fallen. "This hombre still on the loose, Fitz?" Prophet asked him.

Not looking at him, not looking at anything in particular, the sheriff lifted a heavy hand from his chair arm and dropped it. "Reckon," he grumbled.

"Thanks, Fitz," Prophet said, grinning and tipping his hat.

He stepped outside, reading the dodger in his hand. "Five hundred dollars—dead or alive." He turned to his hang-headed horse. "Well, Mean and Ugly," he said, folding the dodger and stuffing it into his back pocket, "I believe it's time for you and me to get reacquainted."

He untied the reins from the hitchrack and climbed into the leather. When he'd pulled into the street and gigged the hammerhead into a trot, a girl yelled his name.

He looked around and saw a scantily clad young woman standing on the second-story veranda of the Queen Bee, leaning on the railing and smoking a thin cheroot. Her long black hair was pinned in a loose bun atop her head. The breeze parted her powder blue duster invitingly.

"Hello, Miss Angie," Prophet called.

"Don't Miss Angie me, Lou Prophet," she scolded. "You're in town and you haven't come to see me!" She set her lips in a pout.

"Oh, I'll be back, Miss Angie," Prophet replied. He

lifted his hat to her, grinning his charming grin. "Don't you worry—I'll be back soon!"

Cantering west out of town, feeling suddenly lighter, feeling spry—amazing what the prospect of a five-hundred-dollar bounty could do for a man's soul—Prophet lifted his head and sang, "Jeff Davis built a wagon and on it put a name, and Beauregard was driver and Secession was the name. . . ."